THE LADY'S KEEPER

The Medieval Ladies Series
Book One

Coirle Mooney

SAPERE
BOOKS

THE LADY'S KEEPER

Published by Sapere Books.

20 Windermere Drive, Leeds, England, LS17 7UZ,
United Kingdom

saperebooks.com

ISBN: 978-1-80055-489-4

For my brother, Brecan, who was like a work of art.

ACKNOWLEDGEMENTS

Huge thanks to my editor, Amy and the team at Sapere Books for their fantastic support at every stage of this journey. My invaluable first readers, Nina and Susan. Special thanks to Dr Ken Rooney, Dr Carrie Griffin, Dr Andrew King and the gang from UCC. Frank and Berry for their encouragement. My inspiring parents, Brian and Noirin, Aunty Mary, Paddy and my precious siblings, Tara, Turloch, Kathy and Brecan. The Monaghan clan. Thank you, Noel, you truly noble fellow.

ACKNOWLEDGMENTS

CHAPTER ONE

Court of Poitiers, 1168

Alice watched as her niece, Lady Joanna, stepped lightly onto the stage. At the same moment, the troubadour, Bertran emerged from behind the curtains and together they bowed before Queen Eleanor, who was sitting on her dais with her ladies. The courtiers were packed in colourful, tight rows on the benches below them.

Eleanor smiled, motioning for Joanna to begin the 'game', requiring her to set a task for Bertran, so he could prove his worth before the court. Joanna's jewel-studded hair, piled high on her head, made her look older than her fourteen years. Her pale, green linen dress was puffed out like a broad leaf and the reflecting light had turned her eyes a fathomless aqua. She looked more enhanced on the stage than her real, neat self.

Bertran had no other course but to be quiet and await Joanna's task.

'On these warm, sleepless nights,' Joanna began, 'I sometimes take to wandering in the woods towards dawn, when moths or butterflies are fluttering towards the morning star and all is shrouded in a white light. I go to the place where the birch trees stand like tall, silent people, lilting their branches to the rhythm of gentle breezes. There I stay waiting for a solitary nightingale to sound his mournful tune. He does not sing for long but shies away to some place out of hearing. When I return to my chamber, I often try to imitate his sweet tones but find that I cannot. More and more these failed attempts press so heavily on my spirits, I am reduced to tears.'

She paused, pretending to wipe tears from her eyes. 'Bertran, here is the task I set for you. I wish to have this nightingale in a gilded cage in my chamber, so I might learn to sing as well as him. I only wish to keep him a short while — until I've learnt from him — afterwards, I will release him again.'

The hall had fallen silent. Alice was staring at Joanna, straining to fully comprehend what she had heard. Had Joanna really just asked Bertran to creep into the woods at dawn and trap a songbird for her?

A prolonged silence followed until Eleanor rose to her feet and said, 'We think the lady sets her lover too stern a task.' Bertran's attendants began grumbling, and an ugly note of dissent was wafting through the hall until the queen spoke again. 'Perhaps the lady could think of a different task to set her lover?'

All eyes turned to Joanna, whose mouth was set in such a stubborn way that Alice's heart sank. She turned in desperation to the queen's daughter, Marie, sitting next to her. 'Perhaps you could suggest they take a break?' she asked. 'Then I could persuade Joanna to change her mind...'

But before Marie could reply, Bertran's loud guffaws sounded round the hall. 'No, no! I would not have the lady change the task,' he cried. 'In fact, I would undertake such a task with relish.'

Alice noticed Marie flinching at the word relish. The queen still managed to look poised as she consulted with her ladies.

'Do you really wish to accept this task, Bertran?' Eleanor asked.

Bertran bowed to her, then turned to Joanna and blew her an exaggerated kiss. 'Lady, I accept your task,' he said. 'You shall have your songbird by the morn, or I am not the famed Bertran de Born!'

An extremely curious court assembled the following evening in the great hall to see if Bertran had succeeded. Opinions were widely divided; many felt that such an impossible task could only warrant trouble, while others held the view that Joanna was right to test Bertran's mettle, as he was a known philanderer. Unsurprisingly, the young ladies tended to side with Bertran, the men more with Joanna, each secretly desiring the attractive mate for themselves. Alice thought it had been an impossible task.

The sound of jingling bells soon stopped their chattering. A group of tumblers with hundreds of tiny bells attached to their bright clothes spilled onto the stage. Their faces were delicately painted to suggest woodland foliage, their necks and heads were crowned with garlands of bluebells and wild strawberries and their sunny garments reflected their playful moods. On their arms were perched noble gerfalcons, symbolizing the hunt. Their awkward acrobatics made clear they were no professional troupe, only Bertran's men dressed up as tumblers, but their funny, failed attempts made everyone laugh.

Bertran was hoisted up among them on a carved throne, resplendent in costly fabrics. His torso was bathed in a fine saffron and ivory mottled silk, resembling glowing marble at first sight, and a twisted wreath of gold cord crowned his head of wavy, nut-brown hair. He was carrying an object which — although draped — was shaped like a birdcage.

Alice slipped out of the hall to fetch Joanna. Noting Bertran's impressive appearance before the admiring crowd, she worried for her niece. Such taste and artistry were in keeping with the queen's ethos, and she regretted that Joanna didn't have her own pretty tableau to present. Too late now to do anything about it; she carried on down the corridor and up the winding stairs to their bedchamber.

She found Joanna sitting up rigidly in front of the looking glass. 'It's time, we must go,' Alice said. 'Are you ready? Let me see.'

Joanna didn't stir and their eyes met in the glass. 'Has Bertran arrived? Did you see him?' she asked anxiously.

'Yes, he's up on stage and everyone is there. We must go,' Alice said, impatiently.

Joanna rose and came forward for her aunt to inspect her. Her russet hair was hanging in free curls down to her waist. Her dress of orient blue had been fashionably slashed to reveal the silver lining, and a thin train of the same silver snaked after her, like an eager brook. Her broad brow showed no disturbance, and her features were serene with the indefinable beauty of youth. No lines, no shadows, no evidence of life's sorrows showed on her face, but all was fresh and smooth.

'Good,' said Alice. 'Try to be composed, good girl, no matter what happens.'

They walked briskly to the back of the stage and parted without a word. Joanna stepped onto the stage.

'Dearest Joanna,' Bertran cried, gleefully. 'See here, I have a little something for you.'

On sight of the cage, Joanna gave a little start as if she had not really wanted — or expected — him to trap the bird.

Dramatically, like a magician, Bertran slowly peeled off the drape. A moment of confusion followed, where all the court blinked and strained to make out what was underneath.

It was a bird all right, Alice soon perceived. It was the right colour, for it was the brown and red of a nightingale, but there was something very wrong. The bird was far too big. Soon, it dawned on her what Bertran had done. He'd dressed up the queen's white cockatoo in common hen's feathers! A joke, of course.

Alice stole a glance at the queen, whose complacent, knowing look revealed she'd been in on the jest. Taking their cue from Queen Eleanor, the courtiers started clapping. Alice looked to Joanna and was relieved to see she too had guessed the joke and was smiling.

'I'm so glad you are pleased,' said Bertran. 'Look! Watch this! I even taught it to sing for you...' He began twittering ridiculously, poking at the bird with his finger, saying, 'Now, you!'

But the bird glared at him, refusing to open its beak. It probably did not like being taken from the queen's airy chamber to be dressed up in hot hen's feathers and paraded before a sea of gawking courtiers to be laughed at. The more desperately Bertran tried to make it sing, the more resolutely it seemed to maintain its silence.

He produced a pouch of fat caterpillars, dangling one before its beak; but before it could consider the bribe, the gerfalcons, peckish and competitive, baited from their perches towards the food. Such a commotion of snapping, squabbling and shrieking followed that Bertran had to call for curtains and the whole thing came crashing to an end.

Joanna had just flopped down — fully dressed — on the bed they shared when Alice entered.

'Oh, what an awful mess,' Joanna groaned, 'but at least it's over now.'

Alice perched on the edge of the bed. 'Turn around so I can unlace you,' she said. Joanna succumbed to her aunt's touch. 'Over?' said Alice. 'What if it's just beginning?'

'What do you mean?' asked Joanna, languidly.

'I don't think you understand, Joanna,' said Alice, sternly. 'This isn't a game. Yes, you and Bertran act your courtship out for their amusement, but he is serious about wanting your hand. You must give him an answer.'

'Oh,' said Joanna, 'I see.'

'No, I don't think you see at all,' said Alice. 'May I ask you something, Joanna?'

'I know you'll ask anyway.'

'Please don't be clever,' said Alice.

'I'm sorry,' said Joanna. 'Do ask me, Alice.'

'Do you actually like Bertran?'

'Ye-es, I like him,' Joanna replied, tentatively.

'Well,' said Alice, grimly, 'I'm not convinced. You had better decide, and fast. The queen wishes to know your intentions towards him.'

Joanna turned around, suddenly animated. 'I like Bertran … but I don't really know if I want to marry him. He's handsome — and skilled and witty and all of that — but I'd like to bide my time and see who else comes along. He is not the only man at court who looks at me. I might have my choice of men! Maybe there's another who would suit me better. I have a notion that when my one true love comes along, I'll not be uncertain about him. I'm not so sure of Bertran, for all his qualities…'

'We all dream of impossible things when we are young, Joanna, but life soon teaches us to be less foolish and to be satisfied with less,' Alice remarked, crisply. 'Now, change out of that dress and wash your face or you'll get pimples.'

'Why should I be satisfied with less?' asked Joanna, seriously.

Alice shrugged. She'd thought the same a long, long time ago, that she'd fall in love and marry. Maybe things would be better for her niece. Maybe she'd have more fortune in love. She could surely do better than Bertran de Born. She'd heard stories about him that she did not like, despite his charm. In a way, the girl was right — why should she be satisfied with less? She did not tell her that marriage and love rarely went hand in hand. She'd find that out herself in time.

At breakfast, the ladies could speak only of Bertran, of his jest, his costume, of his winning smile... Alice noticed with resentment that none of them referred to her niece, who'd not yet joined the table. Alice took a seat next to Marie to try and gauge the queen's thoughts.

'Joanna came to us this morning,' Marie told her, 'to my mother and I.'

Alice looked at her, alarmed. 'But why?'

'It seems she could not sleep last night and went in search of the songbird. She says she waited in the woods all night, but there was no sign of the bird. She was terribly upset; she says she saw evidence that some company had been there. She thinks Bertran and his men must have gone there to trap the bird and — being unsuccessful — either frightened it away or killed it.'

'Oh, that's awful,' Alice said, dismayed. 'The blundering fools. What did the queen say?'

'Well ... Joanna has no cause to lie, and of course if the bird is missing it should be investigated. The woods are protected by law, but then, as it was Joanna who requested that Bertran trap the bird in the first place, my mother has agreed to question Bertran and his men. It will be done quietly, and the worst punishment will probably fall on poor Joanna's conscience, I'm afraid.'

'Poor girl,' said Alice, 'she'll be inconsolable, you know. She really is tender-hearted.'

'I'm sorry for her,' said Marie.

Bertran confessed easily to the accidental killing of the bird and even volunteered to dig it up and give it a Christian burial.

Perceiving how pale and strained Joanna looked, Alice did not reprimand her for going to the queen without her consent. 'What are you doing there?' she asked her, curiously.

'I'm making a shroud for the poor nightingale that was murdered by my vanity,' said Joanna, tragically. 'I'll not have Bertran now and that's for sure!'

Alice turned away to hide her smile.

That afternoon, the queen summoned Joanna to the rose garden. Alice accompanied her and they found the queen sitting on a circular bench before a fecund tree of ruby red roses she'd brought back from the Holy Land. Rooted at its base was a small, carved statue of the Virgin and many offerings — ribbons and trinkets — dangled untidily from the thorny branches. The queen looked striking in a scarlet headdress and linen veil, tied with a jewelled circlet. Joanna and Alice sat beside her and before long Bertran appeared, looking queasy.

'Are you feeling all right, Bertran?' asked Eleanor, peering at him. 'Are you ill?'

'It is my conscience that ails me,' he replied, adding, 'though my heart is in a lot of pain as well. You, lady —' he addressed Joanna — 'are the only one with the skill to cure that sickness. Can you forgive my many faults and accept my love, in spite of everything? Let's put our differences behind us and make up with a kiss?' His words rang out falsely in the natural setting.

'Hmmm.' Eleanor eyed him narrowly. 'Weren't you with your men in the tavern late last night? Perhaps that is what ails you.' She then turned to Joanna with an air of maternal concern. 'So, it's up to you, Joanna,' she said, gently. 'You must tell us, once and for all, if you will have Bertran or not. The decision is your own.'

'I will not have you, sir! By God's teeth, I'll not have you! I'd rather be eaten alive here slowly by snails than have you after what you did to the songbird!' Joanna practically spat the words at him.

Alice started in surprise at the venom in her voice.

'The answer is no, then?' said Bertran, after a pause.

Joanna glared at him.

CHAPTER TWO

The sun was climbing high when Joanna began dancing on the green before an impromptu gathering of courtiers. Her copper hair flew bright and free about her, and the twisting fabric of her dress caressed her shapely form like a loose, second skin.

The sight of her twirling — so provocatively — before the other men clearly maddened Bertran with jealousy and desire, but he was managing to keep his composure. His fake good humour did not fool Alice, and she watched him closely as he whispered with the newly arrived Prince Henry. Tittering, the prince looked back at Joanna critically. Just then, the music ended and Joanna's bare little feet halted abruptly with it.

Alice went to lead her away, but Joanna shrugged her off, irritated. Publicly rebuffed, Alice tried to blend quickly back into the crowd. A familiar sense of aloneness, of isolation, crept over her and she wondered how Joanna could treat her so unfeelingly after all she'd done for her. She watched her bitterly as she laughed and joked with some frivolous ladies on the green.

After Joanna's mother, Alice's sister, Carole had died, Alice had stayed living on their estate to protect Joanna from her brutal father. She'd witnessed the count beating Carole on several occasions, and she knew it was only a matter of time before his vicious temper turned on his spirited daughter. Alice had been in a constant state of fear and had taken pains to keep Joanna out of his sight. Even so, he'd laid into the girl on one occasion, forcing Alice to seek refuge for them both at Eleanor's court.

A shuffling of the crowd alerted Alice to the queen's arrival and diverted her unhappy thoughts. Eleanor, Marie and some attending-ladies swept elegantly up to join Henry and Bertran at the front.

Eleanor addressed the gathering in her authoritative voice. 'We are delighted to announce that there'll be some light entertainment in the hall after the evening banquet,' she said, 'to welcome our son, Prince Henry. Our thanks to Bertran for organizing it at such short notice. We hope to see all of you there for this very special occasion!'

Alice groaned; she was afraid Bertran would use the opportunity to get his own back on Joanna for humiliating him.

That night, a very grumpy Joanna and a weary Alice sat with the queen on her dais in view of the whole court. Alice had pleaded with Joanna to conceal her dislike of Bertran. 'He is such a favourite with everyone, and we are only women,' she'd advised.

'I don't understand why I must pretend to like him after what he did to the songbird,' Joanna complained. 'The worst thing is, Alice, he didn't even seem to care that he had killed it. He showed no remorse.'

'That is the hunter's mentality,' Alice said. 'They go for the kill.'

'Well,' said Joanna, 'at least I found that out before I married him.'

'Yes, so there's no harm done,' said Alice, 'and I hope you will be civil to him, like a lady. He is a man, and he is powerful.'

'Like Mama with Father,' Joanna said, sadly. 'She always had to pretend to be happy even when she was not.'

Alice glanced at Joanna, but she had turned away. She wondered if Joanna knew the extent of the count's viciousness towards Carole and, if so, how had it affected her?

Bertran came on the scene, announcing with false humility that he'd composed a little something for their pleasure. 'I hope it demonstrates,' he said, 'how poetry and music can be such healing arts. As you know,' he continued, his voice thick with self-pity, 'recently, I experienced a terrible —' he paused, apparently searching for the word — 'disappointment in love. It was a huge and sudden blow to the heart. The song I have prepared for you tonight was inspired by this painful event and I hope you, at least, can derive some pleasure from my pain.'

Alice braced herself, not daring to look at Joanna.

He began, 'Lady, since you care nothing for me...' With a voice as silky-smooth as his scarlet waistcoat, Bertran soon had lots of ladies feeling sorry for him and sighing. Alice observed grimly how they cast a cold eye on Joanna.

By the end of the second verse, the serious tone had turned to satire. Alice prayed that Joanna would have the presence of mind to control herself. After suggesting that he create a kind of monster-lady to replace Joanna, borrowing various traits he admired from a variety of women, the rest was a smutty rendition concerning these other women's desirable body parts. The court cheered, delighted that the dear, charming, witty fellow was back in full swing.

Later that night, Alice's troubled mind darted about as she tried to make sense of things. She did not like the way Bertran had stood whispering with Henry out on the green. Nor the cold way the prince had regarded Joanna afterwards — both then and later, in the hall. The image of Joanna dancing so freely came to mind. Her spirit so intact, she was little more than a child. But these men — Bertran and Henry — were so powerful. How could she, a mere woman, protect her from them?

The queen, too, had seemed different in her son's presence. Stiff and coy in her movements. Self-conscious? Anxious to impress her own son? In the hall last night, her ivory throat had been bleeding with rubies, her hair sculpted tightly to her head. Her lips, cheeks and eyes had been touched up so skilfully, she'd seemed again a girl in the full bloom of youth. And none had been as beautiful as Queen Eleanor. Alice had even noticed Bertran's eyes scanning her over slyly, lustfully. The rascal knew no bounds. Why all this effort to entertain her son? Alice wondered. Why all the pomp and paint? And why, Alice worried, was the queen deferring to Bertran, of all people?

Conscious of a light snoring beside her, Alice's breast flushed painfully with the mixture of love and pity she often felt for Joanna. Joanna's free spirit would get them into trouble. She must caution her further. Half-choked with the strain of responsibility, Alice loosened her nightgown at the neck. Tomorrow, she would seek out her confidante at court, Marie, to see if she could shed more light on things.

The comforting thought was dampened by her recollection of noticing a strange man close to Marie all evening. Like the queen, Marie lived away from her powerful husband, but it was hardly seemly for her to be in such intimate proximity with another man.

A violent summer storm confined all the court indoors next morning. At opposite ends of the hall, the ladies took out their needlework while the men sat down to chess. The ladies stole furtive glances at Prince Henry as he settled down to play with

Bertran.

Alice noticed Marie dropping her needlework and stealing out, presumably to meet with the stranger from the previous evening. Alice had learnt that his name was Chretien de Troyes and he'd come to court to stay. Panicked at the news, Alice's heart had skipped a beat, her ears filled with muffled noise. She was faced again with the ugly truth of her aloneness. Was she to lose her only friend to this stranger?

A dark, young widow and a fair girl sitting with Alice had tears of merriment running down their cheeks as they informed her that the meek and scholarly-looking Chretien had been recorded in the pipe rolls as the new Herald-at-Arms. Really, he'd come to court to write, but as the king refused to sanction artistic patronage at Eleanor's court, she was forced to give her artists official, but empty, titles. Any occasion to outsmart the king was cause for mirth among the ladies.

Apart from his joke of a title, Chretien's arrival had gone largely unnoticed, as it had coincided with the arrival of Prince Henry. Prince Henry stood almost six feet tall and was as shiningly beautiful and confident as Chretien was short and humble. He'd inherited his willowy frame, luminous skin, marked cheekbones and burgundy-tinted lips from his mother. He had his father's sky-blue eyes but, unlike the king's ferocious glare, they glowed with a gentle light. His red-gold hair was all his own and hung in long waves unto his waist.

'He's like an angel,' the fair girl next to Alice breathed, 'shame he is engaged!'

'He's married, I believe,' corrected Alice, 'though they don't live together yet as man and wife. His wife, King Louis' daughter, Marguerite, is only eleven years old. But they've been married since they were six and three!'

'Then he'll be wanting some practice, while he's here,' crooned the widow, flashing her cinnamon eyes. 'P'raps I will oblige.'

'I saw him first,' objected the fair.

'What use is a virgin to him?' remarked the dark widow, languidly. 'Better for him to eat of the ripe fruit than of the green... The green will only sicken him.'

'This is hardly a fit debate, ladies,' Alice interrupted. 'Remember you are speaking of the queen's son!'

'Of course, Alice, you are right,' the dark said, carelessly. 'Our feelings for the prince should be confined to the spiritual realm. I'm sure you do not suffer from such base desires, Alice.'

The dark and the fair exchanged a mocking look, their shared, secret joke uniting them maliciously against her.

So, all the unattached ladies would be vying for the prince's attentions that summer. Alice supposed the queen would turn a blind eye, let him have his fun. Why not? She indulged him in everything else.

Shaken by the women's open animosity, Alice laid aside her needlework and went out to the dark, cool corridor. The uneven, cobbled stone felt rough under her thinly shod feet, and she stopped at a slit-like window which gave neither light nor air, but it at least offered a good perspective on the gardens. The gardens were deserted, but ash flung out from last night's fires was swirling about in the wind, refusing to land. The bleakness of the scene made her shiver.

She wandered over to the newest addition to the fortress, the Maubergeonne Tower, which housed the ducal apartments where the queen, her family and their closest attendants slept and sometimes entertained. By day, some troubadours seeking privacy and bright, spacious conditions for their composition were also given access. As Marie and Chretien were not in the gardens, Alice was certain they must be inside. She tried the door but, finding it bolted from inside, she felt the minor shock of some tiny precious thing falling and crashing within her. She was shut out. She did not bother knocking; she had no business there.

She retraced her footsteps back to the great hall and looked about for Joanna.

'She doesn't know what it's like to be young!' she overheard her niece remarking to her companions. Catching Alice's eye, Joanna's speech faltered, guiltily.

'A word, Joanna.' Alice's voice was commanding. 'I was young once too,' she began, once they were out of earshot, 'though it might be hard for you to believe.'

'Of course,' said Joanna, embarrassed.

'You may mistakenly believe those young ladies are your friends, but, believe me, any one of them would sell you for the price of a silk gown. They do not love you, Joanna, they only humour you. You are all rivals for the affections of men, for the status and security of the best marriage you can make. Do not share your tales of woe with them. In order to survive here, we must be strong together. Do you understand?'

Joanna nodded, averting her eyes in shame.

The storm blew over to reveal a tender blue, and a bright sun hung over the afternoon. Cooped up inside all morning, the courtiers were delighted when the queen proposed a hawking expedition. Boots were duly laced and feathered caps smoothed out while the falconer unhooded his birds, affectionately tying bells to their knobbly ankles, while cooing words of encouragement to them. Some of the ladies, Alice included, had opted to wear trousers — more comfortable for riding.

With his hunched shoulders and flapping grey-brown coat, the falconer had started to resemble his birds. Not surprising really, as he spent more time in the Mews than he did with other people. But unlike the birds, whose golden orbs stared unblinkingly at the courtiers, the falconer's eyes were cast downwards in a permanent state of agonizing shyness. It was hard not to laugh at him, especially as the two fluffy goshawks attached to either leg mimicked his movements, shifting their weight awkwardly from one foot to the other.

Alice knew the goshawks well; they were Jean and Paul, the most bloodthirsty pair of predators imaginable, despite their comical appearance. A huge eagle named Flora was perched on the falconer's calloused fist, while a smaller version of the same circled overhead. Eleanor regarded her, quizzically.

'Her name's Fifi and she won't leave her mother, Flora's, sight,' the falconer mumbled. 'It's her first flight so best to let her fly free, keep it natural. She'll learn from her mother.'

'I'll fly Flora myself,' Eleanor said.

When the falconer transferred Flora onto the queen's gloved fist, Fifi immediately began circling overhead.

'Joanna,' Eleanor said. 'Today you shall ride closely by my side and learn from me as this young falcon learns from her mother. I may be an old bird, but I do know a thing or two about gaming and so would you, if you'd had two kings as husbands!' She leant in closer, winking at her ladies. 'Don't leave the hunting to the men. Believe me, you'll appreciate your meat far more when you've had to run after it yourself!'

Alice wasn't sure if Eleanor was referring to hunting the quarry or hunting for a man. She suspected it was both. Eleanor had a clever turn of phrase and often meant two things at once, and it was rumoured that the queen had enjoyed other lovers besides her two husbands.

Sometimes, by her speech, Alice felt the rumours of Eleanor's infidelity might be true. Mostly, though, she thought the queen just enjoyed being provocative. Many of the rumours were so preposterous that it seemed they must have been circulated deliberately to damage Eleanor's reputation, such as the one that claimed she had slept with her own uncle, Raymond of Antioch, while traveling to the Holy Land on pilgrimage with King Louis. Others were more believable, including the rumour that she had enjoyed intimate relations with her present husband's father, the dashing Duke Geoffrey, before marrying his son. And there had been the scandal over the troubadour, Bernard de Ventadour, who'd followed Eleanor to Poitiers, proclaiming his love, penning erotic verses in her name. Henry had been so enraged he'd dragged the troubadour across the sea to his wintry English court. The damp climate and inferior food had made Bernard so miserable he'd soon risked the consequences and escaped back to France.

Once the group had mounted, Eleanor rode out first on her white mare, her splendid hem of embroidered gold glittering in the sunlight and marking her out as the highest-ranking lady. Thanks to her skill at handling the birds, Joanna had been chosen to ride with the first party. Alice attempted to keep her in sight. Joanna's loose, sunlit hair flew brightly beside Eleanor's veil of palest green. Henry and Bertran were riding just behind them, and Alice prayed that Joanna would conduct herself properly. At least there would be little exchange of conversation, as everyone was focused on the hawks.

Eleanor had made it clear that she had Joanna under her wing, and Alice was conscious that she had helped place her there. Alice identified with the falconer who'd placed his precious adolescent eagle in the queen's trust. Like him, she'd be on edge until the expedition was over and Joanna was safely returned.

Pretty soon, Alice lost sight of Joanna. About halfway into the forest the men had followed Jean and Paul through a dense thicket after pheasants in the neighbouring fields, while Flora and Fifi had flown straight through the ancient oak after other prey. The foliage being too thick for the horses, Eleanor and Joanna had dismounted, continuing on foot, while many others — including Alice — returned to the castle.

Alice and Marie stood with their backs to the castle wall, their gazes fixed on the distant forest. Alice was admiring the way evening's golden wand had cast its light over Marie and softened her features. She had inherited King Louis' dark eyes and hair, but also, unfortunately, his prominent nose.

'Joanna will be fine, you know,' Marie said. 'You can't always watch out for her, and you must trust her to make her own way. You have sheltered her well in her early life, Alice, but now she is grown.'

'I know you're right,' Alice said, sighing, 'but she's still so young.'

'I was married at her age,' Marie observed.

'I know,' Alice said, quickly. 'But you are so steady and wise. Joanna, though, is … impetuous and has not yet learnt to control her emotions.'

Marie frowned. 'I'm sure I was neither steady nor wise at Joanna's age, when I was first married. I made many mistakes in those early years, but I suppose I learnt from them. I think it's a shame that we must suppress our emotions all the time. I admire Joanna's free spirit, though I was never brave enough to do as I wished. I believe I'd have lost my mind in those early years if it wasn't for music and poetry!'

Alice detected some sadness in Marie's voice. What girl of fourteen wants to be married off to a stranger and sent to live among his people? Passing in one night from virgin to wife? She wondered why Marie chose to live with her mother instead of with her husband. Her marriage could not be a very happy one. Alice longed to probe Marie, ask her intimate details, but she held her tongue.

Their conversation was interrupted by the sound of bells and horses' hooves.

'They're back!' Marie cried. 'You'll see, all will be well. Joanna has no doubt distinguished herself and won the prince's admiration!'

Alice was surprised; why should Joanna want to win the prince's admiration? The thought had not occurred to her. Marie and Henry were half brother and sister, sharing the same mother, but different fathers. Marie was twice his age; they'd grown up apart and were only recently acquainted, which was why she referred to him as 'the prince' and not 'my brother.' Marie had been brought up at the court of her father, King Louis, in Paris, while Henry had grown up at Henry II's English court and had later been sent to the Archbishop of Canterbury, Thomas Becket, to be educated. His education had just been abruptly halted after a falling out between Becket and Henry II over the way in which members of the clergy were tried for crimes, so Henry was temporarily back at his father's court while the dispute was ongoing. Word was that, he'd be entrusted to instruction by William Marshal, one of the bravest knights in Christendom, whom Eleanor had patronized after he'd defended her honour on one particularly perilous journey from England to France.

Eleanor rode up first, with rabbits and squirrels dangling from her saddlebags. Her attending-ladies' horses were also heavily laden: the hunt had been successful. Flora was proudly preening herself on the queen's arm, while Fifi was circling over Joanna's head. Both girl and young falcon, although dirty, seemed unscathed. The men rode up on their heels and, with a raised eyebrow, Eleanor surveyed their scanty kill. 'My, my, take heed, ladies, if it wasn't for us, we'd go to bed hungry tonight.'

Bertran flashed his strong, white teeth. 'I must have a word with the cook,' he said. 'Better to serve these fat old lazy goshawks for our supper than have them hunt for it!'

Alice and Marie rushed forward, Marie to take Fifi back to the falconer, Alice to take care of Joanna.

Once they were alone, Joanna burst out, 'I've never in my life seen such cruelty; it was bloody murder!' But her eyes were burning with excitement. Alice thought of Marie's advice and did not show how worried she'd been, nor how alarmed she was by Joanna's untidy appearance. 'We — the queen and I — ended up chasing after Flora and Fifi when they went in for the kill — imagine; just me and her alone! It was so hard to keep them in sight, they went so fast, but she said afterwards that I ran as swiftly as a deer!' She was glowing with pride.

'That's wonderful,' Alice encouraged.

Joanna spoke so fast it was hard to follow her. 'I could hardly make out Flora and Fifi; our eyesight is too weak. They have another sense, they feel movement. Everything was the same colour too, the birds, the quarry, even the undergrowth ... all unfolding so fast you have no time to think. That's why they tie the bells to their ankles, so at least we can hear them and get to the kill on time. You have to reward them with a share of the kill — otherwise they might get nasty. Queen

them a rabbit between them, but Flora ate it all
.1ing. I asked the queen why she didn't give them
and she said because Fifi had not killed one herself
1dn't deserve it — we must whet her appetite for the
k1.   1tal, isn't it?'

'Slow down your speech, Joanna,' Alice couldn't help saying, 'and change out of those wet things or you'll get sick, and that'll be the end of your hawking.'

'Where was I? Oh yes,' Joanna said, ignoring Alice's remark. 'You should have seen the way Flora hissed and sniped at Fifi when she followed her after the same prey — that's why I ended up going through the pond with Fifi — the queen said to lead her off another way, or Flora might attack her. So, I went through a pond, but it was so covered in duckweed that I didn't see ... lucky I didn't drown.'

'You went through a pond?' Alice was alarmed.

'It was too shallow to drown in,' Joanna said, quickly. 'As I said, Fifi didn't catch anything, but Flora caught so many — as you saw. The queen is a magnificent hawker,' she breathed, in admiration. 'Still —' she looked disturbed — 'it was like a killing spree. And I felt sorry for the poor rabbits — you could hear them squealing. But Alice...' Her voice lowered to a confessional whisper. 'I wanted Fifi to kill one.'

'Well, of course you did,' said Alice, matter-of-factly, 'you were hawking.'

Joanna smiled gratefully at her. 'You don't think it's hypocritical of me? You know, hating the idea of killing anything, but wanting her to kill all the same?'

'Not at all,' said Alice, kindly, 'if it's about survival. It seems to me like the young falcon's life depends on it.'

'Exactly!' said Joanna. 'The queen said that if Fifi doesn't kill her own meat soon, Flora might attack her, drive her off, or even kill her. I said that couldn't be true, her own mother! But the queen said we had much to learn from nature and that, though nature can be cruel, every living thing has to learn to survive on its own. It's all about survival, and the sooner we learn that the better. She said I had talent and thinks I'll make a really good huntress! Oh, I almost forgot!' Joanna paused, pulling something from her pouch. 'She gave me this lucky charm.'

It was a rabbit's foot, streaked with blood. Alice winced.

'I know it's horrible, Alice; it is murder. And I'll probably have nightmares about those poor rabbits...'

Alice eventually persuaded Joanna to step out of her damp clothes into an evening dress of raw, pale blue silk. They'd been invited to sit with the queen at banquet. Joanna's maid was called to wash and comb her hair into a vigorous new shine and a simple string of freshwater pearls was tied at her throat. The maid observed that she needed no paint, as her cheeks were already flushed pink and her eyes were sparkling as a clear brook.

'You look lovely, Joanna,' Alice said, but she added, 'Make sure your table manners and your speech are as good as your appearance.'

Joanna pouted. 'Have you seen how Bertran eats? Like a pig at the trough!'

'Bertran is no concern of mine,' Alice replied curtly.

'Why do you never dress up?' ventured Joanna, boldly. 'You're not so old, you know. Why do you always wear black?'

'Don't be silly, dear,' said Alice, flashing the rarest of smiles.

'Here.' Joanna offered her a string of Carole's pearls. 'Why don't you wear these? Mama would love you to wear them.'

Alice was touched, but nearly refused outright until she caught the pleading look in Joanna's eye. 'Oh, why not,' said Alice, tying them on.

'You see,' said Joanna, 'they are lovely on you! If you would only do your hair in a chignon and have a burgundy gown made up instead of black…'

'These will do for now,' Alice said firmly.

Eleanor had ordered two meagre pheasant drumsticks to be served up for Bertran and Henry as a joke, while rich bowls of seasoned rabbit stew were passed down the table.

'You must be hungry, Joanna, after all your exercise,' Eleanor said.

'I'm starving! It smells delicious,' Joanna replied.

'Tastes so much better when you've had to run after it yourself,' Eleanor added.

'Oh yes!' Joanna agreed.

'Are you sure you want to eat the murdered meat?' whispered Alice. 'What about the poor squealing rabbits?'

'Oh, don't be so silly, Alice. I meant I was sorry for them being so frightened, that's all. Now that they're dead, it would be a waste not to eat them. At least they died for a good cause.' Joanna's mouth was already full.

Alice wished the queen had not placed them across from Bertran. Joanna was uneasy in his presence and Alice did not like him either. She wondered if the queen was purposely throwing Bertran and Joanna together. If she thought Joanna might change her mind about him, she was wrong, but Joanna now seemed to be a favourite of the queen's, so she probably just wanted her close. Alice supposed Eleanor was attracted to Joanna's temperament and beauty, and especially her free spirit, which probably reminded Eleanor of herself.

Alice cringed when Joanna ignored Bertran's request to pass the breadboard, but luckily Bertran only smirked with amusement. Alice wished Joanna would hide her feelings more.

'What a striking string of pearls,' Bertran said, grinning at Alice. Alice withered down in her seat.

Henry was sitting next to Bertran, cutting his meat off the same board, laughing at his jokes. It was the first time Alice had observed the prince up close, and she regarded him curiously. His manners were elegant, unlike Bertran's, who ate noisily and slurped his wine between loud bursts of conversation. Eleanor's manners and appetites were also refined, and she used her energy to keep up the lively conversation.

'Sign of good breeding,' she said to Joanna, 'a lady who can handle a hawk.'

Henry flicked his eyes across to Joanna, who blushed scarlet under his cool gaze.

Eleanor addressed her son. 'Make sure your Marguerite is well trained in it,' she advised, referring to his child-bride.

It was soon clear from his outgoing manner and his easy speech that Henry was not shy. He gave the impression of being pampered, if well-mannered, used to getting what he wanted. 'The light is so much brighter here,' he remarked. 'England is so grey and dreary by comparison! The weather forces us to be always indoors. And there is so much more to entertain here, compared to my father's court. Such taste and artistry to enrich the senses, lovely ladies to feast the eyes on, poetry for the soul... I'll not want to return, I know. Father will have to come and drag me from here himself!'

Eleanor looked pleased. 'Oh, but he will drag you from here himself, if I know your father!'

'Still,' Bertran beamed at them through wine-stained teeth, 'it promises to be a long, hot summer, and we have plenty of time left to enjoy ourselves. The most we should concern ourselves with is what to have for dessert.'

At that moment, the servers were carrying in colourful jelly sculptures, trays of pastel macaroons and a variety of fruit tarts.

'I know which one I'll choose.' Bertran looked pointedly at Joanna. 'Which of them will you choose?' he asked Henry, gesturing down the table. 'Having tasted most of them myself, I'm happy to advise,' Bertran added with a wink. 'Dive into a soft jelly, maybe, or try a virgin macaroon? Or perhaps a little tart? We've a surplus of those here at court...'

Everyone laughed, even Alice, though she could tell the joke went over Joanna's head.

'I'm sure my son is well capable of choosing his own dessert, Bertran,' Eleanor chided. 'He does not need your advice. But he'll not find any to his taste here.'

'On the contrary, Mother,' Henry said, brightly, 'they look most appetizing. I'd like to taste a little bit of each before deciding which one tempts me best.'

The ladies barely stifled their laughter.

'You may do as you please,' Eleanor said, 'but I'll not deal with your leftovers. Do not bite off more than you can chew, and try not to make a mess.'

CHAPTER THREE

Henry loved jousting more than anything and the biggest tournament ever held at Poitiers was due to take place before his departure. The long evenings were conducive to festivities in the hall almost every night and — as the courtiers loved a saga — this summer it was all about Joanna and Bertran. They just couldn't resist the combination of his worldly charm and her spirited innocence, as he tried to seduce her. Joanna could not understand why they must continue the staged courtship after she'd refused his hand.

'They think he'll wear you down,' Alice explained. 'Until you are betrothed to another, they think he stands a chance. He also believes he stands a chance, but that's due to his arrogance. Remember, they don't know how much you dislike him.'

Joanna had gone to the queen to request that she not be asked to perform with Bertran, given their history, but the queen had dismissed her complaint.

'You must find a way to handle him onstage if you wish to win the courtiers' respect. To back down now would make him the perpetual winner in their eyes,' Eleanor advised.

'Why must I continue to be humiliated by Bertran?' Joanna complained to Alice.

'Don't take it so personally,' Alice remarked. 'Remember, it's only a game.'

'Well, what if I refuse to play?'

'Joanna, we are not in a position to refuse the queen anything. We must go along with her wishes. At present, her main preoccupation is the entertainment of the prince, and you and Bertran are expected to play your parts. She is not worried about your feelings, and we must comply with her wishes. If she asks you to jump through rings of fire with Bertran, you must jump.'

'It already feels as though I am jumping through rings of fire,' grumbled Joanna. 'They are all on his side; they call me a cold-hearted prude behind my back.'

'I have been called much worse,' said Alice. 'You'll get used to it.' But Alice had noticed that Joanna's nerves were fraying under the strain, and she knew they would both be glad when the summer was over. Joanna was quieter these days and was not sleeping well. Often when Alice woke in the night, she'd find the bed empty beside her. She cautioned Joanna not to wander out into the woods as it could be dangerous, but she couldn't make a prisoner of her either. 'I thought you loved to perform. Cannot you just imagine Bertran is someone else?' Alice suggested.

'I don't care for singing since Bertran murdered the songbird,' Joanna said, darkly. Petite in her pearly-coloured dress, her face was made more beautiful by pain.

Alice did not know what to counsel. 'Come here,' she said.

As Joanna moved across the room, her lithe form radiated energy. Alice adjusted the white lace trimming on her bodice.

'All ready?'

'Yes,' Joanna replied, cheerfully enough.

Alice was glad to be kept occupied as chaperone to Joanna. She felt isolated since Marie had taken to spending time with Chretien de Troyes. Alice had been drawn to Marie the moment she'd set eyes on her, when she'd been lined up in the hopes of being included in Marie's courtly retinue. Impatient at how long she took with each applicant, Alice nonetheless watched Marie with fascination. Never before had she observed so open and animated a face. She watched her easy laughter, her sudden frowns, with surprise and interest. When her turn had finally come and she'd found herself before Marie, Alice had stood silent and quivering. Marie had kindly advised her to sit and take her time.

Unaccustomed to niceness, Alice had to swallow her tears before she could speak. Finally, her tale of suffering and woe at the hands of Joanna's cruel father had gushed out and she had begged Marie for a means of escape from his household — more for her niece than for herself. She spoke of Joanna's beauty and breeding, her talents which surely they could use at court? Marie had promised her refuge there and then and even offered to help make the arrangements. Joanna's father would be paid in gold and assured that his daughter's talents would be nurtured at court, where she would certainly meet a husband of breeding and wealth. It was an offer no ambitious father could refuse. Relief had flooded through Alice. The strain of protecting the free-spirited Joanna from her vicious father had been becoming too much. Marie was the first person to offer her respite from the years of struggle since Carole's death.

For the first few months, Alice had been shy of Marie, but it was impossible not to come into close proximity over time, and they became slow — but true — friends. Their shared sensitivity allowed them to understand each other easily, and they valued each other's opinions in the often self-serving atmosphere of the court. Until Chretien had arrived, Alice had been Marie's closest confidante, but Chretien had upset the balance, making Alice feel redundant. His sensitivity was equal to Alice's, while his cultivated mind was a much better match for Marie's, so what use was she to her now? Alice had the sensation that she was physically shrinking, while Chretien was growing larger, more substantial by the day.

Chretien's arrival forced her to realize how emotionally reliant she'd become on Marie and when Marie seemed oblivious, the hurt was like a choking, angry smog about her heart.

Alice was surprised, therefore, when Marie and Chretien sought her out that evening to ask if she would help them paint a set. Her effort to distance herself from the pair of them was no good, as they lived at such close quarters. She had no choice but to challenge Chretien for Marie's affections. What other joy or comfort did she have in life? The steady fire of their friendship burned in Alice's breast with a new intensity.

'Chretien would like to portray some scenes from his stories,' Marie explained.

'That sounds ... interesting,' said Alice, stiffly, 'but I don't see how I could help. I'm no artist. Anyway, Joanna needs my assistance.'

'Oh, Joanna is fine,' said Marie. 'You'll still have plenty of time to help her before tonight. Besides, it will do her good to fight her own battles. We only wanted to borrow you for a few hours, didn't we, Chretien? Please, Alice? I wouldn't ask, but we really need an extra pair of hands...'

How could she resist those lively eyes? At least Marie was including her, even if it meant being thrown together with Chretien.

Alice planned to make her escape as soon as possible, but she soon became absorbed in Chretien's storytelling. In a soft voice, he spoke about a powerful knight named Lancelot who had to rid the kingdom of an evil enchantress living in the forest. Alice had never heard such fantastic tales and she soon forgot herself, letting the brush slip from her hand.

'Bravo!' Marie clapped at the end. 'You see, Chretien, I told you she'd be spellbound!'

Alice flushed, picking up her brush. 'Oh, I'm sorry, I couldn't help listening...'

'No, no, don't apologize.' Marie grabbed her hand. 'That is exactly the kind of reaction we were hoping for.'

Marie's smile was like basking in sunlight, and Alice felt her insecurities melt away. She realized she'd been wrong to avoid Chretien. She'd have to try and make friends with him, if she wanted to stay close to Marie. She offered to help them all week, if they wanted.

When the curtains were drawn up on the painted scenes a week later, the courtiers fell silent with wonder. Alice exchanged smiles with Marie across the room. The audience was spellbound as one of Chretien's stories about the feats of the knight named Lancelot was acted out by players and accompanied by musicians.

'Bravo!' Eleanor cried after. 'Bravo!'

All the court rose to their feet, clapping and cheering their praise. Chretien was lauded as a genius.

With everyone still in high spirits, a game was proposed. Some young men and ladies — including Joanna — were blindfolded and sent to wander among the painted scenes. After much confusion and laughter, they managed to pair themselves off, removing their blindfolds and revealing their identities.

It seemed Joanna had been paired off with the prince. The musicians struck up a tune and the couples started dancing.

Alice felt the touch of a hand on her back. 'Oh, Marie!' she exclaimed, swinging around. 'Chretien must be so proud!'

'He is,' said Marie, 'but he is shy and has run off! Come with me?'

Alice followed Marie past the dancing couples, through the curtains to backstage, where they found Chretien at a table, a large parchment spread out before him.

'Look at this,' said Marie. 'It's Chretien's new narrative. We are working on it for next week. We've had a little disagreement over this part; what do you think?' Marie pointed the section out to Alice.

While painting was one thing, Alice could neither read nor write and apologized with great embarrassment. Marie asked for forgiveness for her assumption and insensitivity, while Chretien assured Alice that it mattered not one whit whether she could read or not. Despite their kindness, Alice felt humiliated, as they'd discovered how shallow her intellect was compared to theirs.

In bed that night, these thoughts prevented Alice from sleeping. She kicked off the sheets, lying on her back with her eyes absorbing the darkness. Her ears tuned into the sound of distant laughter emanating from the great hall. These dances sometimes went on all night. Debauchery was the word which sprang to mind. *Joanna!* She'd forgotten all about her!

She pricked her ears and focused on the distant noise. Before long, she heard footsteps coming swiftly down the hall. She was relieved when Joanna's silhouette appeared in the doorway. She breathed easily again, shutting her eyes.

'Alice, are you awake?' Joanna whispered.

Alice did not reply, but let her breathing sound deep and even, as though she was asleep. She wanted to be left alone with her thoughts.

Joanna sighed, hopping in beside her in her undershift.

Alice woke to fierce sunlight burning through the shutters and saw that Joanna had already risen. She'd missed breakfast, no doubt, maybe even lunch, but she didn't care. After last night's festivities, many of the courtiers would lie in bed all day, nursing sore heads, rising only for the evening banquet, which they'd all be expected to attend. She'd have preferred to spend the whole day — and night — alone. At times like this, she wished she'd lived a simple, solitary life in the countryside, but she'd not have been able to sustain it. And who would have looked after Joanna, then, after Carole died? Joanna would certainly not have been content to live with her aunt in isolation! Besides, court life suited Joanna, with her beauty and her talents. In this she resembled her mother, who'd always been the popular one.

Alice rose quickly and went to wash. Despite the heat, she dressed head to toe in crisp black and braced herself for the day ahead.

The great hall had two stages: the main one, which was used for performances and games, and a smaller, intimate platform which was used for light entertainment during banquets. This stage was lit by poppy-dyed candles which gave out a foxy hue, as well as opiate fumes to pleasantly stimulate the senses.

Alice gasped with the others when Joanna made her entrance in an alarmingly transparent gown. Eleanor's idea, no doubt; Alice would never have allowed it. It was completely inappropriate for a girl Joanna's age; it suggested experience, not youth and innocence. A train of burgundy feathers had been attached to her behind like the luscious tail of a frisky cat, and it swished now — sensuously — as she danced. Alice's cheeks burnt with shame as the courtiers whooped their encouragement. In their eyes, Joanna was there to entertain them, no different from a courtesan, with no parents to protect her.

'May I?' Bertran sat down heavily beside Alice. She resented his manly bulk infringing on her space. 'A delightful girl, your niece,' he grinned. 'All the men think so.' He picked up his knife and stabbed a piece of meat; the backs of his fingers were hairy. He leant in so close she caught the sour whiff of beer on his breath. 'How long, though,' he continued, conspiratorially, 'before all of this —' he gestured towards the stage — 'goes to her head? If I were you, I'd advise her to settle down and marry before she is ... well, spoiled. This kind of display is bound to give some men the wrong idea, and who could blame them? As her guardian, I'm sure you would agree it would be best to take her out of harm's way. Despite a certain obstinacy of nature — which I would quickly correct — I would still be willing to take her off your hands, to marry her, but my offer only stands so long as she is pure.'

Alice did not reply but stared coldly ahead as Bertran put forward his case, speaking between large mouthfuls of food. The abundance of rich meat and heavy wine was off-putting to Alice's more delicate appetite, and Bertran's coarse manners — not to mention his speech — was making her feel queasy. She observed with fierce dislike that there was no difference between his enjoyment of his meat and the way he was currently viewing Joanna — as fresh and tender flesh. In her heart, though, she knew Bertran was right; a girl as alluring as Joanna did not stand a chance among so many predators. How could she have allowed herself to be tarted up like that? But then she remembered telling Joanna she must do as the queen wished.

'If anything were to happen, you'd be accountable in a way, wouldn't you?' Bertran calculated, pleasantly. He suggested they strike up some deal between them, but Alice had stopped listening. Her attention had turned to the other end of the table, where Marie had taken her place. She was shimmering in black and silver. Alice wished their eyes would meet, but Marie's eyes were fixed gravely on Joanna, whose dance had just ended. The girl looked pleased with herself, and her eyes searched eagerly for the queen, who beckoned her over.

Marie has forgotten my existence, thought Alice.

Barely conscious that Bertran was still speaking — through mouthfuls of roast stork — she excused herself absently and rose to leave, deciding she could stomach neither the food nor his company a second longer.

'Go, you go,' Bertran agreed, jovially, 'and don't forget our chat.'

Alice noticed his eyes were already looking past her as he spoke, and she followed his gaze to some painted ladies who'd just alighted in the background like bedraggled, exotic birds after a long flight. Prostitutes. The queen turned a blind eye to them, but Alice — and Marie — found their presence offensive. So, Bertran would satisfy himself with these tough cuts tonight, while he waited for more tender fare to come. Alice guessed that he would feast just as happily on either. She'd be damned before she'd encourage Joanna to marry him; she'd be hanged from the scaffold first.

Why was it, she wondered, that Bertran's promiscuity was deemed 'normal' while any woman who behaved in the same way would be branded a whore? The men could go with prostitutes while Joanna would be deemed impure for wearing provocative clothing. The awful injustice of it — and the sticky heat of the hall — caused Alice's head to throb fiercely.

She dragged herself to bed, closing her eyes to ease her pounding head.

CHAPTER FOUR

Alice woke up early and was glad to find Joanna beside her. One of Joanna's legs was thrown outside the covers, and her shiny hair was pooled messily around her. The irreverent posture irritated the neat and tidy Alice. Her eyes fell on the tail of burgundy feathers draped across a chair, so animated last night. She rose and dressed quickly, wishing to be out in the fresh air as soon as possible.

She strolled along the empty corridor and stopped briefly at the slit-like window to check the day. She loved the long, cool corridor, especially this early in the morning when no one was about. She always stopped at the same window, with the best view of the gardens, and she liked to contemplate while looking on the roses, so pleasing to the eye, soothing for the soul. The day was dewy and overcast, a welcome respite from last week's heat. Her mood was also lighter, less foreboding.

In the hall, any remnants of last night's entertainments had been expertly cleared away, the boards newly set for breakfast. All seemed fresh and new, as if to match her mood. Just as she was settling down to enjoy her quails' eggs, a guard near the doorway shuffled to his feet, alerting them to the arrival of an important personage.

A moment later, the queen, her ladies and Marie came sweeping into the hall. It was an unusual appearance; normally Eleanor breakfasted in the Tower with her attending ladies and did not make her first appearance till after noon. Their clothes were strangely dark, even drab, perhaps to match the weather, but Alice was struck at how youthful Eleanor looked, younger even than Marie.

While the party arranged themselves, Marie beckoned to Alice to join them.

The ladies joked about the night before, and Alice soon learned that Joanna had drunk too much. Alice blamed herself; she should not have left, but should have stayed to watch the girl. *How long before all of this goes to her head?* Bertran had warned.

Alice was grateful for Marie's secret, sympathetic glances, as the other ladies gossiped. Alice was not often at such close quarters with these ladies. Two of them were fashionable Parisians who'd come from King Louis' court, while the other two spoke with English accents, having come from Henry's court. One of the English ladies, a tall, fair beauty, did not seem to realise that Joanna was Alice's niece, and she began to speak uncharitably about her.

'There has been too much frivolity lately,' Eleanor interrupted her, tactfully. 'Lady Rosemary, your own goblet was never empty last night, I observed. Nor did you shirk from having our troubadours refill it for you. Why should you? They are handsome and you are eligible.'

Alice smiled, gratefully.

'It is time we gave something back,' said Eleanor. She addressed Alice. 'We are planning an expedition today, to the abbey of Fontevrault. That is why we have risen and descended early. You see, the day is cooler and more suitable for riding, and we must take advantage of it. I was just about to send for you and Joanna, for you must come with us, of course. It's a long ride and I know Joanna will be tired, but only God knows when we shall have the chance again. A messenger was dispatched at dawn and the nuns of Fontevrault will attend us before nightfall, God willing.'

Alice marvelled yet again at Eleanor's energy — she could not have been in bed before the bell struck twice, and to be up again at dawn, planning a journey…

'We shall stay ten days or more. Plain, dark clothes and veils are most appropriate; make sure Joanna is equipped. We shall congregate in the courtyard on the chime of nine.'

Alice had some job explaining the queen's rash plans to the muddled, hungover girl. Finally, Joanna understood, but to Alice's irritation, she did not rise at once but stretched herself out luxuriously and began to chat.

'I had such a wonderful evening,' Joanna said, dreamily. 'I so love dancing. You know, I think it's absolutely my favourite thing. I danced all night, Alice. You were fast asleep by the time I came to bed! It was growing light outside, and the birds were singing. I was tempted to go into the woods and listen to the dawn chorus, but I know you do not like my going there. Did you see my costume, Alice? Wasn't it sumptuous, with all those beads and sparkles and that exquisite tail…?' Her eyes darted around, looking for the feathers. 'There it is!' she cried, gleefully, spying it on the chair. 'She said I could keep it as a souvenir … and Alice, I had so many compliments; I think I could have had my pick of any man there!'

'Joanna, please, it's immodest of you to speak like that,' Alice said, sharply.

Joanna's eyes flashed with dislike. 'I'm sorry Alice,' she said, slowly. 'I don't mean to be vain, but it's so hard not to be when everyone tells you how beautiful you are, and all the men are staring at you all the time. It was wonderful. Oh, my head hurts! I drank a little too much, but I don't mind,' she added, carelessly. 'I had such good fun.' Her expression was faraway, dreamy.

'Well, I *do* mind,' said Alice, but she wasn't too cross. Joanna's joy was infectious, and she was glad to see her happy again. Besides, both Marie and the queen had suggested that she might be being overprotective of her — that she should allow her more freedom. Joanna was no fool. So, she did not reprimand her for the costume, or the drinking, but she did remind her that pride comes before a precipice.

'Don't forget that beauty does not last; it's only an illusion. It is your character that is your real asset, Joanna. In the end, that is what lasts and that is what people remember. Make sure your habits and your actions are good and moral, and do not mistake compliments on your looks for compliments on your character. They are not the same thing.'

Slightly subdued, Joanna rose and started to prepare for Fontevrault. She moved behind the dressing frame, where Alice had hung her clothes. Only her head peeked out above it, and her grey-blue eyes focused brightly on Alice as she became suddenly pensive. Joanna's mood could change as quickly as April weather. With her usual directness, she asked if it was true that Fontevrault was a refuge for battered women. Alice said she'd never been there, but she understood it was just such a refuge and everyone knew that the queen was devoted to the abbey.

'Some of her younger children live there, don't they?' Joanna asked. The queen had nine children with her present husband, King Henry, as well as two daughters by King Louis of France. She'd borne her last child only three years ago, at the age of forty-four. Alice said she'd heard that this youngest child — John — had been sent to Fontevrault to be brought up in the Church, perhaps as a future bishop. It was customary for great families to offer one of their children to the Church and as John would have no land, it would be a good career for him.

'What a sad, strange environment to grow up in,' observed Joanna. 'I'll seek him out and play with him, poor boy! But I suppose the nuns have become his family, the same as the other courtiers have become ours.'

Alice checked to see if she was in earnest. Alice did not think that the other courtiers were like family, but she said nothing, glad if Joanna felt an inclusion which she could not feel herself. Apart from Marie, Alice trusted no one at court.

'Do the nuns of Fontevrault have lands for hunting and hawking?' Joanna asked. 'They never would allow it, would they, being so holy?'

Alice said she'd never thought about it, but she supposed they'd have to live as well as everyone else.

'Perhaps they make the battered women do the hunting for them?' suggested Joanna, smiling mischievously.

Alice was not so curious about the customs and habits of the abbey. If there was any way she could get out of the trip, she'd gladly take it, but she'd have to go, at least to chaperone Joanna.

Joanna needed help wrapping the linen veil around her head. Unmarried young women were not normally required to wear them, so it was new to her. Silently, Joanna handed Alice the gold circlet — which had belonged to Carole — to fasten it in place. Alice winced in sorrow, but secured it firmly, giving Joanna's shoulder a small, affectionate squeeze. The girl's eyes filled with tears, like deep rock pools. Perhaps — the thought struck Alice — this was another reason why Joanna was so eager to please the queen. Alice herself was no substitute for Joanna's charming mother, but Eleanor had all those qualities that Joanna most esteemed.

Alice surveyed her work proudly. The veil framed Joanna's apple-shaped face, and without any paint she looked like any other fresh-faced maid. A different creature altogether from last night's little vixen.

'I'm looking forward to meeting the nuns,' Joanna said, sweetly, 'and the other women who live there…' Her voice was suddenly sad. 'Poor Mama should have gone there, shouldn't she, Alice? But Father wouldn't have allowed it and then … it was just too late.'

'Let us not think of it now,' said Alice, quickly, feeling the familiar wrench of grief on her heart.

It seemed Joanna had been more conscious of her father's brutality than Alice had realized. Well, that explained why Joanna never asked after her father. The girl had such poor male role models, it was no wonder she was not in a hurry to marry.

'I wonder if we'll be residing with the queen — and Marie,' Joanna said, brightening up. 'I doubt it, do you? I wager they'll be in some gorgeous apartment of their own and we'll be shoved into the same room as all the other ladies!' Joanna averted her eyes, suddenly embarrassed. 'I have heard that even prostitutes are not turned away from Fontevrault. I cannot believe it, though — how could such women live side by side with holy nuns? It is not right, if it is true, but I doubt it is.'

'There are things we don't understand,' said Alice, 'and it's better not to judge.'

'Oh, I don't mind,' said Joanna, eager to sound grown-up. 'If there are such women there, I'll speak with them the same as any other.'

They were a party of twelve, including Eleanor and Marie. A knightly escort would go ahead to protect them from ambush by thieves or robber-barons. The courtyard was a hive of busyness, with groomsmen and their boys tending to the mares and the knights eyeing up the ladies, who met their glances discreetly.

The ladies took a competitive pride in their individual mares, seeing their horse's glossy coat and tail as a reflection of themselves. Each horse was inspected with a critical eye before being greeted by its owner. The queen's horse, Hero, was brought out last, and with some ceremony, for she was an exquisite creature of the palest pearl and stood hands above the rest — said to be descended from the warrior-horses of ancient Rome. All stood back as Eleanor mounted, flashing a glittering hem which blended perfectly with Hero's coat.

Snail slime, Alice suddenly remembered — that was what the queen allegedly used to keep her skin looking so youthful!

A falcon hovered, haltingly, overhead and Joanna recognized her hawking companion. 'Fifi!'

All their eyes gazed up at bird, until the falconer's whistle recalled her. Joanna ran up to him for a quick word about the young falcon. Afterwards, when she'd mounted, he shouted, 'She'll need to make a kill next time, lady, or her mother will drive her off.'

'I'll see to it!' Joanna called back with confidence. Even heavily veiled and wearing a grey smock buttoned to her neck, Joanna did not fail to attract the furtive glances of the knights, much to Alice's dismay.

Despite the queen's hopes of reaching Fontevrault that night, they ended up staying at a minor castle en route, which was encircled by a deep — but parched — moat. Set in remote countryside with a generous river running through it, they stopped to survey the cows grazing idyllically in the lush surrounding fields.

Joanna found the silence eerie, but Alice loved the peace that it invoked. Tired out from the day's riding, the ladies went to bed straight after they had eaten. They were — as Joanna had suspected — all sharing the same room, some sharing the same bed, except for Eleanor, who had a room elsewhere. Marie whispered to Alice that she could not sleep on a full stomach among so many dozing ladies and wondered if she'd walk the grounds with her.

The castle grounds were marshy and unkempt, but their wildness was pretty and mysterious in the gloaming. They hardly spoke, but Marie took Alice's hand and they listened to the music made by crickets. An owl screeched plaintively, with haunting clarity, and they both marvelled at the sound.

'Isn't it romantic?' said Marie. 'It is such a pleasure to walk with you, Alice. My mother — God preserve her — does not stop talking and giving her opinion on absolutely everything! And her energy is indefatigable — it is exhausting.' Marie gave a peal of nervous, but merry, laughter.

They both knew that Alice could not comment on the queen and were happy to let a gentle silence fall, with only the sound of their feet crushing the long grass beneath them. Alice snuck a glance at Marie, but dark mist had shrouded her features.

'You know, I was a terrible disappointment to my parents when I was born,' Marie confided. 'They were hoping for a boy, of course, to secure the inheritance. I was whisked off to the nursery out of sight and sent to a convent to be educated at first opportunity. I hardly remember seeing my mother as a child.'

'How sad,' said Alice.

'Not at all,' said Marie, merrily. 'I received a wonderful education and for that I shall be eternally grateful. That is the only reason I can read French and Latin; I would never have had the patience to teach myself!'

Alice guessed that Marie was kindly making up for embarrassing her the other night with Chretien.

'That is why I am relishing this opportunity to get to know my mother, even if it is exhausting at times. There is one thing I do regret.' Marie's voice became wistful. 'I'm really sorry that I've never known my half-siblings. Prince Henry is like a stranger to me. I hoped we would be friends, but I see now it's too late.'

'Perhaps there is still time?' said Alice.

'Oh, I don't think so,' said Marie. 'He's to return to England at the end of the summer, and I've hardly spoken to him. I'll probably not see him again for years, if I do ever see him again in this life.'

CHAPTER FIVE

The party was up again at cock's crow, sitting down at a long table. Their hostess had spread the table generously, and Eleanor advised them to eat up before the ride ahead. Rich dairy cheeses and plates of pork were passed down the table with baskets of freshly baked breads. Their hostess encouraged them to wash down the food with steaming, creamy milk, instead of the usual ale.

'I never serve ale to ladies, only good, wholesome milk from our own dairy cows,' the lady of the house proclaimed. 'That's how my mother brought us up and I've had three fine sons and two pretty daughters mature to adulthood. Ale's not good for the reproductive system, you see, milk's much better.'

The sweet scent of milk was sickening to Alice so early in the morning — she'd have much preferred a small cup of ale to settle her stomach. But Joanna was drinking it greedily and the hostess complimented her on her appetite, saying she'd make some lucky lord a pleasant and fruitful wife. Alice and Joanna exchanged a secret, mocking look. A true gossip, their hostess entertained them with anecdotes about the squires, farm hands and maids about her land, but, she added, with a sudden, dark change of tone, only last winter they'd had a terrible tragedy. One of their milkmaids — 'a delightful child with rosy cheeks and so skilled' — had drowned herself in the flooded marsh. She added, with a barely perceptible flicker of pride, that the girl had drowned herself for love of her son. Of course, it was inconceivable that a lord would marry a milkmaid — how she got the idea... A terrible business, parents were inconsolable, poor things. 'A fine girl, very skilled,' she said, practically, 'hard to replace, you know.'

Alice and Joanna exchanged impatient looks and rose to leave the table.

'Awful woman,' Joanna muttered.

They returned to the dormitory, each of them deeply troubled by the story.

Alice thought of the milkmaid's skilled, plump hands — now skeletal — at work on her cows, drawing the milk down, perhaps talking to them as she worked. The smell of hot milk squirting into the pail, the girl's hands all sticky sweet, patting her hair back into place. Thinking of her young lord, fancying that this very milk might line his stomach, secretly delighting in this small, sensory connection between them. She probably fancied he loved her back, of course. What had happened, then, to drive the milkmaid to despair? Had she confessed her love and been rejected? Had the young lord used her first then scorned her? What had caused the rosy-cheeked maid to end up drowned in the marsh?

She thought back to the boy she'd once loved who'd fallen for her sister.

'What a waste,' Joanna exclaimed, bitterly. 'She must have been a fool, to throw her life away like that.'

Alice had taken the story particularly badly. *Why?* she wondered. 'Maybe you will understand it more when you fall in love,' she said, quietly. 'Love can make people do strange things.'

Joanna turned to her, suddenly pale and quivering, her eyes cloudy with anger. 'How do you know I've never been in love? Why do you presume to know everything about me, Alice? I do not assume to know your secrets.'

Stunned by the outburst, Alice stared at her.

Joanna went on in a low, menacing voice. 'And I know you do have secrets, Alice. I'm not a fool ... and I know you'd rather die than tell me. Why do you think that I am any different from you? Why should I not have secrets, too? I have no one to confide in since Mama died. You are always so quick to judge me. Sometimes I feel I cannot breathe around you.'

'You are not yourself, Joanna,' Alice said, quickly. 'Our hostess's story upset you. I understand; it has upset me too. Take some time to calm yourself. Go and wash, you'll feel better. Don't worry, I forgive your outburst.'

It was not the first time Joanna had surprised Alice with such an outburst, but it had never been so violent and Alice felt quite shaken.

The ladies rode all morning and, after mounting a steep hill, the abbey of Fontevrault came into view below them.

The massive abbey walls were as thick as tree trunks, and it was roofed with dark oak beams, giving a sturdy, indestructible impression. In contrast to the main, austere building, two quaint white chapels were attached at either end and many small outhouses were dotted about haphazardly.

Surrounding it on all sides were miles of oak forest, as well as vines, olive trees, fruit trees and land for vegetables. Goats and cows grazed in the smooth, outer pastures. Above all, it seemed like an oasis of peace and prayerfulness.

Despite her weariness, Alice smiled. It seemed to her a wonderful sanctuary away from the heat, noise and corruption of the court.

At Fontevrault, the ladies untied their saddlebags and were shown to a dormitory and invited to choose their beds. Each one (apart from Alice) secretly missed the bustle and entertainment of the court and hoped the ten days would pass quickly. The bleak, unfamiliar dormitory unsettled them, and as they unpacked they caressed their things for a bit of comfort. Sensing the dreary mood, Marie made a little announcement, suggesting that they walk the beautiful grounds till supper.

'I suppose the queen is having sweet wine with the abbess now, while we're expected to fast all day!' Joanna hissed.

'Or, alternatively, you could join my mother for prayer in the west chapel,' suggested Marie, as if she'd heard. 'The east chapel is used by the monks.'

An astonished murmur went round; they had not realized that the abbey housed monks as well as nuns!

'Separately, of course,' Marie explained, grinning. She seemed embarrassed, on her mother's behalf, for dragging them all from the comfort of the court to this stark, serious place. 'Please feel free to view this as an adventure,' she said, apologetically, eyeing Joanna, the youngest member of the group. 'I always find that a week at Fontevrault does wonders for the spirit. I must advise, though, that you experience your spiritual awakening quietly.' Marie's eyes twinkled. 'The nuns demand silence at all times, and running on the grounds is also completely forbidden... Apart from that — and all the hours of obligatory prayer and fasting — you are free to do as you please!'

'Why did the queen take us here?' Joanna groaned, but Alice did not reply. She was lying flat on her bunk and could feel herself drifting off to sleep.

When Alice woke, she was surprised to find she'd slept away the afternoon and the ladies were already lining up to wash their hands before supper. Marie's face was bent to hers.

'I'm so sorry I dragged you out late last night,' she said. 'I can see you are tired today.'

Alice sat up quickly. 'It's not that,' she said, 'it's the story our hostess told this morning; it upset Joanna strangely and we had a disagreement after.'

'Shall we walk down together?' Marie suggested.

The meal was basic and punctuated all the time with prayers led by the abbess, who sat beside the queen. A powerful, widowed noblewoman, her corpulent body was sheathed under a starched, white habit and an oversized, gold crucifix hung down from her waist on a chain, sometimes clanging against the dishes. At first, the newcomers confused the sound with the prayer bell, which was shivered delicately between courses. Overall, nobody spoke much or, if they did, only in whispers so that the meal was like a quiet meditation in itself. Alice found the silence comforting, but Joanna was restless.

Afterwards, Joanna and Alice sat together on a stone bench in the cloister and admired the peachy softness of the evening. Normally so anxious, Alice welcomed the brief respite from the busyness of the court, while Joanna was excited about exploring the grounds. They both preferred to forget their earlier quarrel without comment.

'I think I've made a friend,' said Joanna.

'Already?' said Alice. 'My, that was quick!'

'While you were sleeping, I went to explore the grounds. I saw a group of nuns. They stopped to inquire who I was, and when they were satisfied I wasn't an intruder they went on their way — all but one. Her name is Sister Heloise; she is only about my age, imagine! She said she'd grown up here at the abbey and was destined to serve God. But she was so curious about Poitiers and wanted to hear all the stories of the court, so we stayed talking until the supper bell rang. We arranged to meet tomorrow at the same place. She is really nice, Alice, not at all like the ladies at court.'

Poor Joanna had been deprived of friends, really, as she was less worldly than the other ladies, who were either older or wary of her as a rival.

'I could really talk to her, Alice,' Joanna said. Then, as if she did not want to hurt Alice's feelings, she added, 'You can come with me tomorrow, if you like, Alice. I think you would like her too.'

Grateful for the little kindness, Alice thanked her, but said she thought young people should be left alone together. Joanna was clearly relieved.

By the end of the ten days, both Alice and Joanna were sorry to leave Fontevrault. Between the complicated task of protecting Joanna and the unpleasant spectre of Chretien de Troyes upsetting the balance between herself and Marie, Alice dreaded returning to court life. The fantasy of Fontevrault was really her desire to build a fortress around herself, Joanna and Marie, a defensive wall to keep out the men who threatened to divide them. She knew it was unchristian, but what other source of happiness did she have? Joanna was devastated at leaving her new friend, the young nun. The two clung to each other pathetically on parting. Joanna wept dramatically and they swore to write, promising their eternal friendship.

'Don't forget our secret,' Alice heard Joanna say to the young nun.

'I wish I could take her with me,' Joanna said to Alice. 'I'd give anything to have a friend like that at court. How awful to be brought up as a nun; I'd hate it. Imagine being cooped up here for life, never seeing the outside world, never dancing or hunting or … kissing a boy.'

'Yes,' Alice agreed, but she was thinking that the court was an institution too, just one with looser morals. In lots of ways, they were as restricted as the nuns. None of them could move outside the court unchaperoned and if a lady was attacked, she was deemed responsible. Even when it came to marriage, they were bound to be arranged for political gain, rather than love. If a powerful duchess like Eleanor could not manage to free herself from under her husband's thumb, what hope was there for the rest of them?

'Who is to say your friend would be happier at court? She seems to enjoy her life here,' Alice suggested.

'Oh, I'm not saying she'd be happier, I'm saying I'd be happier if she was there!' Joanna remarked.

Eleanor mounted first; they had not seen much of her over the ten days, as she'd spent the time in deep prayer and fasting. She looked astonishingly rejuvenated. Joanna and Alice trotted behind the others and fell into conversation.

'So, what is this secret that you spoke of with your friend?' Alice inquired. 'And what would you know about kissing boys?'

'Oh, nothing much,' Joanna answered breezily, 'only that I kissed the prince at the last banquet!'

The news hit Alice like a shower of hail. Her reaction was severe. 'He is a married man, Joanna! Where are your morals? You did wrong. What will people think? I am ashamed of you.'

'You see,' said Joanna, bitterly, 'that is exactly why I didn't tell you before, but then, foolish me, I thought that we understood each other better after our quarrel and you would listen to me, for a change. Foolish, foolish me for trying to confide in you, Alice. You don't care about me at all. You only care about what other people think.'

'I don't care about you?' Alice was shocked. 'You don't mean that, Joanna. How can you say that after all I've done for you? After all the sacrifices I've made for you?'

'What sacrifices, Alice?'

'What do you mean? I've sacrificed everything for you. I have cared for you, fed and dressed you, protected you. I am always worrying about you.'

'You can feed and care for a dog, Alice. I need more. I've had no one to love me since Mama died. Any time I try to speak to you about something important, you silence me or judge me. You never even hug me. I feel so alone sometimes I could die! The truth is you had no life to sacrifice. Where would you have gone after Mama died, if you had not stayed to look after me? Without me, where would you be? I've said nothing before out of respect for Mama and pity for you, but do not expect me to be grateful for the security I have given you.'

'How dare you speak to me like that, child. I have means, I am a count's daughter, the same as you!'

'I am not a child,' said Joanna, sternly. 'I turn fifteen next week. I am old enough to be married and bear children, and if I want to kiss the prince again, by God's teeth, I will.'

'Do not swear!' Rage swelled up in Alice's chest as Joanna rode off, constricting her breathing and rushing to her head like a swarm of bats. How dare the girl speak to her like that!

CHAPTER SIX

Alice and Joanna settled back into court life separately. Alice's rage sustained her resolve to ignore her niece's comings and goings, while Joanna went about seemingly oblivious. Underneath the anger, Alice was conscious of a hurt, like a cut, which grew deeper each time Joanna ignored her. She was frustrated too that this distance had occurred just at the time when her watchful eye was needed most. She suspected that Joanna might have done it purposely to accommodate her passion for Prince Henry. It was no secret that Joanna was in love with him. She never had been able to conceal her feelings, which was a dangerous flaw in a young lady at court.

When Joanna dressed now, it was clearly with Henry in mind.

'Well,' Bertran exclaimed when Joanna entered that evening in a new dress made for her birthday. 'Just as the flower opens its petals to attract the bees, so the maid displays herself to attract the boys.'

The remark was typical of Bertran, being both lewd and charming, but Alice noticed that his eyes were hard. Henry barely lifted his eyes to look at Joanna; if he was in love, he was doing a great job of hiding it.

Alice observed them all from across the overheated room. The new dress revealed what Alice had taken pains to conceal; Joanna had come of age. All eyes in the room landed on her like bees on lavender. It touched Alice with a sense of loss. Carole had been a beauty, too.

Joanna's rich, auburn hair had been swept into a thick side coil, and her face was a delicate palette of peaches and rose, with her eyes glowing like fiery moonstones. The dress hugged her small frame like the golden-striped fur of a lively young cat. Perhaps the most surprising thing of all was the long, curled slippers which shod her usually bare feet, the same kind worn by the queen.

Joanna's smiles were aimed at the prince. And yet, it disturbed Alice that Henry barely looked at Joanna, while all the others stared — or tried not to stare. Likely he was spoilt, used to the attentions of beautiful young women. Joanna seemed oblivious to his indifference, while doing nothing to hide her own infatuation.

An open book, thought Alice, *an open heart... Possibly, an open wound to come?*

Over the course of the evening, Alice drew herself into closer proximity with Henry. Despite his flawless manners, she found him hard to read. Surely if he was really devoted to Bertran, he would not have kissed Joanna? Everyone knew that Bertran was still lusting after her and would do anything to bed her. Alice was certain that Bertran cared nothing for Joanna, really, but was obsessed with the hunt. When she observed Henry hanging on Bertran's words, laughing at his jokes, it seemed that he loved the rogue far more than Joanna.

Up close, Henry's complexion was as fair as a girl's, his cheeks as rosy, and his hair was the most extraordinary shade of red shot through with gold. His light blue eyes shone with depth and his nose was fine, yet strong, while his lips were expertly carved.

'Well, well!' Bertran had noticed Alice staring; his voice startled her out of her reverie. 'Are all of the family greedy for a piece of royal pie?'

Alice tried not to blush. 'Just sticking in the thumb, testing to make sure it will not sicken my niece,' she said, with humour.

'If she grows big after eating it, I daresay it'll sicken her every morning!' Bertran joked.

Alice bowed to them both before turning away, but she noticed how Henry looked her fleetingly up and down and then dismissed her, as all men did. Alice had long stopped caring about what men thought of her, but Henry's face had stirred up the memory of a time when she was barely older than Joanna was now, when she and Carole had fallen in love with the same boy.

The young lord had stayed a summer in their father's house to attend a tournament, and he cut a fair, fresh figure, with his snowy-white hair and the colourful tunics he wore. When he smiled, both sisters swooned, so he soon guessed his power over them. When he chose Carole over Alice, even though Alice was the kinder one, it was the first time she realised that she might not be attractive to men. The worst thing was that Alice knew how much more passionately she would love compared to Carole, but that did not seem to matter to the boy. All that summer, as Carole discovered first love, Alice sank deeper into misery. Finally, she became so despondent that her parents sent for the physician, who confirmed that Alice's health had deteriorated, though he did not know why.

Her parents had no clue as to the torments of their daughter's heart and soul, and so her illness remained a mystery. No one noticed when her recovery coincided with the young lord's departure at the end of the summer. But the experience had altered her and she had aged, mentally and physically, the bloom of youth disappearing from her cheek forever.

Mistaking Carole's superior beauty for entitlement, she began devoting herself to her sister's needs, forgetting her own. In this way she placed a guard around her heart, to avoid further hurt. Almost overnight, she turned from being outspoken and lively to being largely silent and withdrawn. So, while Carole blossomed into a real beauty and was admired and courted by many, Alice became her meek little helper. She grew so accustomed to the critical, dismissive eye cast over her by Carole's lovers that finally it caused her no pain. She learnt to view men objectively, as if there was a barrier between them, so she could not be hurt.

But the buried memory of her first love had caused a disturbance in her like muddied water, and she needed to be alone to settle her thoughts. These days, as preparations for Henry's late-summer tournament were underway, Alice and Joanna shared their chamber with any number of surplus guests. The outdoors was therefore the only place where she could be alone.

Alice was aware of two conflicting feelings; the first was her instinct to protect Joanna from the same hurt that she had experienced; the other was the sense of frustration that Joanna — like Carole — might experience the fulfilment of a love that she had been denied. Either way, Alice concluded, life was unfair. She was certain her heart and soul had been as beautiful as Carole's, so why had she not received equal love? Even their parents had preferred Carole and seen Alice as a burden. Joanna clearly did not love her either. Tears sprang up hotly from her anguished soul as she made her way blindly out into the night wilderness.

She was surprised to hear Joanna's voice calling out to her.

'Alice, I came to find you. We've not been friends, have we?' she panted, catching up. 'Would you shake hands with me?'

Speechless, Alice was flooded with relief. She was glad of the darkness hiding her tears. She held out her hand for Joanna to clasp.

'I want to show you something,' Joanna said. She was carrying some kind of bundle. 'Eleanor gave it to me!' she said with excitement. 'It is one of her old hunting tunics. We can take it back and spread it on the bed, if you like?'

The material was leathery green, almost like toad-skin. It consisted of a tunic and pants, with elaborate, fitted underpants which made them laugh.

'What on earth...?' Alice struggled with the mess of entangled straps attached to the underpants. 'It seems this thing must be strapped on to your thighs and waist, then all these tiny buttons have to be fastened to the pants to hold it in place. Well, well... It is old-fashioned.'

'I was hoping you could help me into it, Alice,' Joanna confessed. 'The queen said I must wear it tomorrow ... when we go hawking with the prince.'

So, that was why Joanna had suddenly started speaking to Alice again; she needed her help. 'You are going hawking with the prince?'

'Not only with the prince! There is to be a small party of the best hawkers.'

'Well, I was not invited,' Alice said, feigning insult. Her brain was working fast; this was the first time Joanna would be unchaperoned. She said nothing, afraid of rupturing the moment. 'Well, no one could get into this outfit by themselves!' Alice said with a smile. 'At least you will be well protected.'

'The terrain is so rough that Eleanor says I need a proper hunting outfit for protection. I am to fly Fifi again and this time she must make a kill, as you know, or her mother will drive her off. So, I'll probably be dragged through all kinds of undergrowth, like last time…'

Alice thought it irresponsible of the queen to put so young a girl at risk, but she held her tongue.

'Alice, I have to tell you — if I don't tell someone, I'll burst!'

Alice braced herself. Whatever it was, she mustn't scold.

'I am in love with the prince!'

'Yes, Joanna, I know you are.'

'How do you know?'

Everyone knows. 'By the way you look at him.'

'Oh,' Joanna said, 'do you think he knows?'

'I think he may have guessed,' said Alice.

'Oh! Well, it's true, everything I do is for him. I had this dress made with him in mind. Do you like it, Alice? You know, it was strange going to the dressmaker without you.'

'I like it very much,' said Alice.

Joanna squeezed her hand. 'I love him, Alice, I've never felt this way in my whole life.'

Fifteen whole years! thought Alice, wryly.

'I think about him all day long. I imagine talking to him and telling him all my secrets; I imagine him telling me his. He is the only man at court who does not stare at me, but I believe he loves me too. He does not love his wife; that was just arranged when they were children. Everyone says he does not love her. He's so beautiful, so good and he deserves my love.'

Alice had once felt the same herself, until life with all its disappointments had knocked her flat. The prince's indifference seemed plain enough to her, but perhaps Joanna was drawn to him because of his indifference. Poor Joanna would learn the truth soon enough. 'I'm happy for you, Joanna, you know I am,' she said. 'Just be careful.'

'Oh, thank you, Alice, wonderful Alice! So, I can count on you to help me in the morning? I must return to the hall now. Would you like to come back with me? The dancing was just starting when I left…'

But Alice went to bed, happier than she'd been for weeks.

CHAPTER SEVEN

The tunic gifted to Joanna was rough, edged all around with coarse, gold thread, but the overall effect was striking.

'You look like a princess out of the old legends!' Alice exclaimed, delighted. Her fingers were tingling from all the tiny buttons.

'Well!' Joanna exclaimed. 'I do feel transformed! Imagine, Alice, I'm wearing a costume that the queen wore! But I'm afraid she was much smaller than me! She must have been tiny.'

Late for the call, they rushed out to the courtyard where the knights, ladies, horses and groomsmen had all assembled. They cast their eyes furtively over Joanna, before turning back to flirt or to inspect their horses. The falconer was standing in their midst, his arms extended as perches for his birds like feathery appendages. The birds were calmly preening themselves, pausing now and then, haughtily, to return the courtiers' stares.

The falconer allowed Joanna to handle Fifi, so they could reacquaint themselves before the hunt. Alice stood beside them, sharing in Joanna's admiration, her excitement. Alice was again conscious of a strange affinity between herself and the falconer, knowing that neither of them would be at ease until their charges were safely returned.

The crowd dispersed to make way for the queen's horse, Hero, her head held high and knees kicking up, as though aware of her lofty lineage. Henry and Bertran arrived together, comically wearing identical hunting garb. Eleanor halted before Joanna to inspect her and gave a nod of approval. Joanna curtseyed prettily, while Alice bowed her head. When Bertran approached, Alice moved off to avoid him.

Alice shielded her eyes to check the horizon. Pale, grey clouds were hanging like a heavy duvet across the sky, sealing in the afternoon heat and casting a glaring light. A nearby water trough was a rife breeding ground for mosquitos, whose thin drones were amplifying maddeningly close to where Alice and Marie stood.

'Come inside, Alice,' Marie implored. 'We'll be eaten alive if we stay here.'

Alice did not budge, her eyes fixed on Joanna. 'Why were you not invited to go with them?' she asked. 'Why did the queen take such a small party?'

'I was invited,' Marie said, 'but I don't really enjoy the sport, as you know…'

'I don't really enjoy it either,' Alice sighed, 'but Joanna loves it. She emulates the queen in all things. I should have insisted on going with them.'

Marie smiled at her. 'I know it is useless for me to say so, but you really mustn't worry about Joanna. My mother loves her. She will not let her come to any harm.' She placed her arm around Alice's shoulder, guiding her inside.

Alice spent a delightful day in Marie's company, losing all sense of time until the melancholy baying of the hounds and the watchmen's warning shouts brought her back to reality.

Everyone rushed out to greet the returning party, but the excitement turned to horrified silence when they spotted a body stretched across the queen's horse. Bertran and Henry appeared to be missing.

'Joanna!' Alice shouted, breaking into a run.

'No, Alice!' Marie tried to catch her arm, but she broke free.

Eleanor halted as Alice approached wildly. She was her usual, composed self, apart from two bright red spots on her cheeks.

'Joanna! Oh, I knew it, what happened to her?' Alice's voice was strangled with fear. 'What have you done to her?'

'This woman has taken leave of her senses,' Eleanor snapped. 'Men!'

Just as the men-at-arms rushed forwards, a swirl of feathers engulfed them all. The falconer appeared from out of nowhere, his ragged coat flapping, and the birds of prey landed on him like a tree.

Alice was pushed back roughly, while Joanna was lifted down and propped up. She was alive, but she was a mess of blood and mud, her clothes ripped, her breasts exposed and dripping with marsh weeds.

'Cover her up,' Alice begged, tearfully.

Eleanor wrapped her own veil around Joanna. Joanna was mumbling something. 'Fifi,' she was saying, over and over.

The falconer's eyes were searching anxiously around… Fifi was missing.

Alice watched silently, keeping her peace. She'd feared the worst and was relieved to find that Joanna was at least alive and capable of speech. Her hair was matted with dried blood, one eye half closed and purple.

Eleanor sent for the court physician. She said a knock to the head had occurred when Joanna had fallen off her horse. But why were her clothes all torn like that? Why was Bertran missing? And the prince…

The physician bowed to the Queen, then took Joanna's pulse and peered into her eyes. He frowned, breathing heavily as he looked her over. 'The lady's head must be shaved,' he said, after a while, 'in order for me to examine it thoroughly.'

'Oh, her hair!' The ladies gasped.

He turned to the queen. 'A thorough examination of this lady must be carried out, in private.'

'Of course,' said Eleanor. 'Everyone go inside. The girl shall be taken up to my own bedchamber immediately.'

It was understood that a thorough examination meant checking to see that Joanna was still a virgin. Her reputation was already ruined, of course. Everyone would be afraid to speak the truth. But the rumours would be ruinous to Joanna's prospects; a raped woman was considered damaged goods.

Later, alone and feeling utterly helpless, but grateful not to have been arrested for her outburst, Alice recalled how Bertran had cautioned her to let Joanna marry him, 'before it is too late.' He had warned her, too, that she would be considered responsible if anything happened to Joanna. She was tormented by the thought that it was all her fault; she'd failed to protect her niece. She had brought her to the castle to escape the brutality of her father, but she had instead subjected her to a worse kind of brutality. She had failed to protect her sister's child and she had underestimated Bertran's viciousness, his influence over the prince.

But the worst torment was the thought of her niece being attacked. Little more than a child, it was unbearable to think of a man — or men — forcing themselves on her. The terror and violence inflicted on an innocent spirit was as evil as murder.

Alice's waves of grief were interspersed with black rage. She had placed Joanna in Eleanor's care, and Alice was suspicious of the role that the queen had played in the tragedy. Had she not ensured that Joanna would be without protectors on the day? Had she not set her niece up for the fall? Anger and suspicion blew up such confusion in her brain that she

71

resolved to go and see the queen first thing in the morning and demand some answers, even if it meant imprisonment.

The brilliant sunshine seemed to mock her mood as Alice leapt out of bed next morning. She paused in the corridor to look out at the garden, bathed in glorious, morning light — perhaps for the last time. The vibrant, high summer purples and deep pinks caught her eye, but failed to lift her spirits. Her eyes took a moment to adjust back to the dim-lit corridor as she carried on briskly to the Tower. The doors were bolted from within, and she hesitated a moment before pounding on the solid wood.

Footsteps quickened on the other side. 'Who's there and what's your business?' a guard's voice called.

'I am Lady Alice, Lady Joanna's aunt, and I request an interview with the queen,' she called back.

'Hold on.'

After some muttering, the door was unbolted and Alice was invited to step inside. It was her first time inside the Tower. She found herself blinking against the light, in a gallery with high ceilings. Inside, some men-at-arms were standing casually around.

'Lady Alice, you must wait here while we send your request to the queen,' one of them said.

It was after noon before they returned for her, giving Alice ample time to reflect on her misfortunes. She noticed how much happier a place this seemed than the older part of the castle which they inhabited. Bitterly, she thought of the unhappy circumstances that had led them here. She had always suspected that some dark fate awaited her. For Joanna, though, she'd hoped for something better.

When the guards came, she was staring vacantly at the mosaic patterned floor. They led her up a broad, winding staircase with narrative tapestries hanging down the walls. Unlike the mean, narrow stairwell they climbed up to bed, these stairs could comfortably accommodate three or four people walking abreast; a queen and her attending ladies.

'Come in, Alice. I am sorry to have kept you waiting,' Eleanor called.

Alice was shaking with fear, but determined to speak her mind. On sight of the queen, she faltered; Eleanor was still in her nightshift, and her face was slathered in a greyish mask of mud.

'Please excuse my appearance, Alice,' Eleanor said. 'I am not young anymore, and I need my rest and this mask or else I look a fright! It is a pressure to be always in the public eye.' Her voice was quieter, less commanding than the one she used in public. 'Please sit, Alice. I am so glad you've come to visit. You could have come before, you know. We have known each other long enough now, I think, to consider ourselves friends?'

Alice nodded; she had not expected the friendly tone. What nonsense, she thought, that she'd have been welcome here before. 'Joanna...?'

'Of course, you've come to inquire after your niece. Joanna is doing well, just a few scratches, really, and a bang to the head. The physician has assured us that she is still intact.'

Alice could not believe how nonchalant Eleanor sounded, how bold she was. Anger began rising in her again and she had to take a deep breath to calm herself. 'Intact?' she picked up, carefully. 'You mean she is still a virgin? Forgive me, my lady, but who would believe that she is still a virgin after what we witnessed yesterday?'

To Alice's amazement, Eleanor looked more amused than upset. 'You are right, Alice. Nobody would believe she is still a virgin after yesterday. Everyone will assume that she was violated, especially since Bertran has run off.'

'But ... who would have her now?' Alice said in disbelief. 'Who would want to marry a lady who is not a virgin?'

'Very few,' Eleanor agreed, 'but, I assure you, Joanna was not raped. She's had a shock, that's all.'

'A little more than a shock, I'd say,' said Alice. 'I saw her with my own eyes. Everyone saw her, the condition she was in!'

Now Eleanor showed some discomfort, shifting in her chair. 'Alice, sooner or later, someone was going to take her. You were no longer able to protect her. You really know nothing about men, do you, Alice?' Eleanor sounded weary. 'Talk to Joanna, she'll tell you herself she was not violated.'

'Still,' said Alice, grimly, 'her prospects of a good marriage are ruined, are they not? Won't that impact gravely on her future?'

'And on your future?' said Eleanor. Alice blinked. 'I agree that tongues will wag and Joanna's reputation may be damaged, for a while. But Alice, believe me, most of the most powerful ladies have a story in their past and in time, if Joanna proves herself, it will be forgotten. Trust me, I am speaking from experience!'

'If Joanna proves herself? But she did nothing wrong? She's only a child. It is we who have failed to protect her!'

'I know she did nothing wrong, but that's not the point. Don't be naïve, Alice, you know Joanna is not entirely innocent. I love the girl, but people will say that she's too headstrong and was bound to get herself into trouble. That business with Bertran and the songbird, for example...'

'But how will she bear the shame?' asked Alice.

'I've thought of that,' Eleanor said. 'I agree it would be difficult for her to carry on as before, and she'll certainly want to avoid Bertran. That's why I want to invite you both to live here in the Tower — as my attending ladies.'

Alice stared into Eleanor's violet eyes. Attending ladies to the queen!

'If you accept my terms, I will guarantee your protection. We can say your niece is traumatized and that your presence by her bedside is required. That way, Joanna does not have to appear in public until she feels ready. All I ask for in return is your loyalty, to me alone. I do not ask that you are loyal to the King, or to the princes, only to me. That is all I ask of my attending ladies. If you do not wish to swear fealty to me, you and Joanna are free to leave and take up residence elsewhere.'

'Why us?' Alice managed to ask.

'I see a lot of myself in your niece,' Eleanor said, 'and my daughter, Marie, tells me that no one is as discreet, as "subtle-souled" as yourself, Alice. I need this kind of discretion for what lies ahead.'

It seemed to Alice they'd been left with little choice, and it was a much better prospect than what she had imagined that morning. 'We are at your service, my lady.' Alice bowed her head.

'That's good,' Eleanor said, 'and in time this thing will blow over, but for now you are under my protection. You may move into your new apartment at once, if you like. I'll send for your things.'

CHAPTER EIGHT

Alice was touched by how vulnerable Joanna looked with her shorn head, but resisted the urge to pat her hand over its fluff. Joanna had lost all desire to be seen in public and was tired and melancholy. Her puffy eye and swollen cheek were causing her pain, and Alice was kept busy applying poultices or linens soaked in rosewater. For the first few days Joanna ate little and slept most of the time, while Alice tried to comfort her.

'What happened, Joanna?' she ventured, but Joanna would just turn away and cry.

'Please, please, I don't want to talk about it. Oh, I am so ashamed.'

'Don't worry about your hair, it is growing back already,' Alice said. 'It only serves to emphasize the beauty of your face.'

'Oh, it is awful! My crowning glory gone! I was so beautiful just a few days ago in my dress... Now look at me, I am ruined.'

'You are not ruined, dear, you will be as good as new again quite soon.'

Joanna's melancholy worried Alice, but she did not probe her, hopeful that she'd confide in her own time. She was certainly cured of her lovesickness for the prince.

The queen visited them diligently every day to check on Joanna, sometimes with Marie. Although they were confined now to the Tower, Alice felt freer than ever before. With its bright, ogival vaulting overhead and green and gold circular tiling underfoot, their apartment on the third — and highest — floor was a little replica of the queen's own. In winter, heat from her fires would rise to keep them warm and they would enjoy creature comforts they had never known; a welcome change from the often gloomy conditions they had shared with the courtiers on the other side. Alice was surprised at how considerably the new environment brightened her mood. Slowly, she became more relaxed around the queen, although she still found her speech cryptic.

As Eleanor often slept late, they'd been advised to tiptoe around their apartment in the mornings. Alice loved to sit on a cushioned chair beneath the window, watching the changing morning light stream in. But her favourite time was late in the evening, when she would contemplate the moon, pouring like a golden egg into the deep blue sky, knowing they'd not be disturbed. Joanna still slept most of the day and cried. It did not help that Prince Henry's tournament was currently underway and shouts of merriment were resounding round the grounds.

One morning, Joanna sat up in bed and peered at Alice's needlework. She was refreshing one of Joanna's winter dresses by adding a white lace collar.

'I am no longer the sweet young thing I was,' Joanna remarked, 'so my dresses should be cut low from now on.' Her tone was bitter.

They both jumped at a knock on the door. Eleanor entered, dressed in a night gown of midnight blue velvet, with pink, cut-out stars and a long, pink train. Her hair was hanging in a thick braid down her back. Before, they'd never seen her casually attired like this; they'd hardly even seen her without a headdress or veil. Now, they were getting used to seeing her in various states of undress, which Alice found embarrassing.

'Oh!' Joanna exclaimed, sorrowfully. 'Your hair is so lovely against the blue! Our hair is exactly the same colour! Though I don't have mine anymore…'

They both had rich, russet hair; Joanna's was just a shade darker.

Eleanor squeezed Joanna's shoulders. 'I'll have one just like it made up for you for Christmas,' she said. 'Your hair will have grown back by then.'

Joanna thanked her with an adoring smile. Alice's heart faltered like a broken wing; Joanna never looked at her like that.

'You've been here some weeks now,' Eleanor said. 'I hope you find your new apartment comfortable.' She explained to them how the Tower had once housed her grandmother, Dangerosa. The rectangular keep, with its four, decorative turrets was built by her grandfather for her grandmother, out of love. Her grandfather, Count William IX, was thought to have been the first troubadour and in a grand, romantic gesture he'd added on the Tower to house his mistress, Dangerosa — Eleanor's grandmother. The Tower was named after her — Amauberga, or 'the Dangerous.'

Joanna was impressed, but Alice found the story shocking, particularly as Dangerosa had been married to the Viscount of Châtellerault and had borne him three children, when William had run off with her. It was widely believed that the Count had abducted Dangerosa from his vassal the Viscount — who'd been too afraid to come after her. William's wife, Philippa, had been outraged when she returned to find Dangerosa in her home, but William refused to give her up. He even had Dangerosa's portrait painted on his shield, with the notorious statement that, "it was his will to bear her in battle as she had borne him in bed." Philippa retired to Fontevrault, where she was said to have died of a broken heart.

'Why was she called Dangerosa?' asked Joanna.

'My grandmother was a grand seductress,' Eleanor said. 'With just one look, she could steal the heart of any man. But she loved my grandfather deeply, and he loved her. So, I was begot of passion, not politics, as so many are.'

It struck Alice that Joanna's parents, too, had married for love. Out of her many admirers, Carole had chosen Joanna's father because she loved him, but he'd turned out to be brutal and she'd ended up a prisoner in her own home. It was said that the Tower had been a kind of gilded prison for Dangerosa too; William had kept her like a songbird in a cage.

'Of course, my grandmother was no fool,' said Eleanor. 'She would not settle for being William's lover. A noblewoman gains power only through her children, and she ensured that her offspring would inherit Aquitaine. Within one year of Phillipa's death, she'd persuaded William to betroth his son and heir — also named William — to her daughter, Aénor, ensuring her own bloodline's inheritance. Dangerosa may have been passionate about Grandfather, but she was even more passionate about Aquitaine! So, you see, I was called after my mother, Aliénore — "the other Aénor." When Aénor and William's son — my brother — died, my father brought me up as Aquitaine's future Duchess. He had his vassals swear fealty to me on my fourteenth birthday! Thankfully, Aquitanian law — unlike anywhere else — allows women to inherit property in our own right and to rule over it autonomously. My father always said that my spirit was akin to Dangerosa's, and I believe that my son, Richard, has the same spirit.'

Eleanor paused, eyeing Alice and Joanna narrowly to make sure they understood. It was no great secret that Eleanor wanted her third and favourite son, Richard, to inherit Aquitaine. Her husband had still not agreed to this and wanted young Henry to inherit it as well as England.

'We are not the lords of Aquitaine, we are its guardians,' Eleanor said with passion. 'But my husband does not seem to understand the difference. And he wonders why the barons continue to rebel and why he has endless trouble from this land? Aquitaine does not need to be ruled, it needs to be nurtured. It is not French; it has a different soul, a different culture, even a different language. It is a poetic land and its history, its song needs to be sung, free from constraints…. But Henry refuses to see it!' Her voice had risen in anger. 'Forgive me,' she said, 'it is just so maddening. Henry continues to ignore all of my advice and, as everyone knows, he ties my hands by trying to govern Aquitaine from afar. Power has gone to his head, of course.'

'You are powerful,' said Joanna, 'but it has not gone to your head!'

'Thank you, my dear,' Eleanor said, 'but I am not so powerful now. Indeed, my father would be disappointed with me for relinquishing Aquitaine. But Henry is impossibly strong and stubborn, and I was so desperately in love with him. It's true that love is blind.'

'Yes,' said Joanna, flatly, 'love is blind.'

Eleanor and Joanna exchanged meaningful looks. Alice wondered what she was missing.

'You know he has a mistress that he loves more than me,' Eleanor continued, 'who he wishes to be with more than me… She's terribly young.'

Alice was amazed to see Eleanor's eyes suddenly fill with tears.

'I am Aquitaine's bloodline Duchess and even after my annulment from Louis, Aquitaine was returned to me. No King — not even Henry — can separate me from this land. I would never have married Henry if I'd known that he would try to take it from me.'

A sudden cheer from outside seemed to applaud her speech and they all smiled, grimly.

'My son's tournament,' Eleanor said. Joanna flushed.

Alice was delighted to be missing it. They'd heard that Bertran had skulked back from his stolen castle just in time for it.

Eleanor picked a handful of dried rose petals from a bowl, breathing in their fragrance absently and letting them fall through her fingers. 'I hope you won't be bored much longer,' she said. 'Henry will return to England, where he is to be ensconced in his own castle with his own retainers. My husband and my son, Richard, are arriving on the same ship that will take young Henry home. Richard will come here to us in Poitiers, but my husband will go to his castle at Chinon and stay there until Christmas. Bertran, too, will return to his castle for the winter, and you will be able to move about freely again, Joanna.' Alice watched her slender, gold-ringed fingers nervously kneading the petals. 'The castle of Chinon is the artery of royal intelligence, as well as the King's favourite estate. It is so vast and has such a multitude of entertainers who ply their trade there that Henry knows few of them by face. One clown is employed the whole year round just to fart before the court at Christmas! To meet demand, Chinon has its own Marshall of the Whores!' Her expression was one of amused disgust. 'Alice, you are looking at me quizzically, thinking "what does this have to do with us?"'

Alice, who hated being addressed directly, flushed horribly. 'Uh, no,' she croaked, clearing her throat. 'It's all very interesting ... although Chinon sounds like a dreadful place... I was not wondering...'

Eleanor laughed lightly.

'I think it sounds interesting,' Joanna said, 'with all those entertainers, it must be very lively.'

'Maybe you shall attend me there at Christmas,' said Eleanor, 'then you shall see it at first hand.'

Alice's turbulent brain kept her from sleeping that night. She gazed at the sleeping girl beside her, so small and childlike, especially with the shorn head. She'd seen a look in her eyes, while Eleanor was talking, a hard look; Alice realized that something about Joanna was different. Had something died in her that day when she had lost the young falcon? Had she been raped, after all? Could she really trust Eleanor to tell her the truth? Could she trust anyone at all?

'Joanna, come sit with me for just a moment,' Alice said the following morning.

Joanna came, but she was rigid with reluctance.

'I feel I'm losing you, Joanna,' Alice blurted out. Both their eyes welled up with tears.

'Can you tell me what happened to you?'

Joanna's chest heaved and a torrent of tears gushed out.

'Were you violated?' Alice asked.

Joanna shook her head then changed her mind, nodding. 'Oh, Alice, I am so cold.'

Alice wrapped a fleece around the shivering girl.

'I was violated, Alice,' Joanna said, 'though not in the way you think. My love was violated, and I felt danger all around. For the first time I understood that there is real evil in the world.'

'I understand, Joanna, I have felt it too.'

'Fifi felt it too,' Joanna whispered. 'I could tell by the way she was screeching when it was happening.'

'When what was happening, Joanna?'

Then it started tumbling out so fast Alice could barely follow.

'I'd followed Fifi through a thicket, and we were separated from the others,' Joanna began. 'I wasn't scared because the same thing had happened before. I'd tied my horse to a tree to go faster on foot. Then, I heard my name called out and when I turned around, I saw Prince Henry coming towards me. He was so beautiful it seemed like he was shining, Alice. His hair was all lit up by the sunlight, and he seemed so tall and fair. I thought he'd followed me there because he was in love with me.' She covered her eyes in shame. 'Oh, I've been such a fool! I'm too ashamed to say it.' She turned away, so she didn't have to look at Alice. 'I fell into his arms and started kissing him. I even undid my own bodice, so he could feel my breasts. It's so stupid, Alice, but I wanted him to think I knew what I was doing. I wanted him to be mine. But when he started pulling on my tunic, I got scared and told him to stop. I tried to guide his hands back to my breasts, but he pushed me down and tried to pull down my undergarments. He was stronger than he looks and he was different, all worked up, and I was really scared. I could hear Fifi screeching all the time.

'He'd pinned me down and I don't think I'd have stood a chance, only then Bertran shouted out, "That's enough." There was all this laughter and I saw that the other men were watching all the time. They'd been hiding in the bushes, and Henry knew that they were there because he said something about how he'd have won the wager if it wasn't for all those damn buttons.

'Oh, Alice, I'm so ashamed. I felt so stupid. I was so angry I hit him, and he struck me back; that's how I got the black eye. Then, I spat at him and he said I was disgusting and to run along if I wanted. He cared nothing for me, Alice. I thought he loved me! I saw hatred in his eyes when he looked at me, that's when I felt the evil. So, I ran and ran until I got to my horse, and I was so blinded by tears I fell off my horse and I forgot all about poor Fifi. Then, when I remembered and went back for her, I couldn't find her. Eleanor brought me back. She asked if I'd been violated and I told her no but nearly, and she said she'd been nearly violated herself and I'd get over it eventually. Which I suppose is true. But I'll never love again.'

'I thought it was Bertran,' said Alice.

'Everyone probably thinks it was Bertran,' said Joanna, 'but Bertran actually saved me, though he was in on the wager. I've been thinking, maybe I was too hard on Bertran. Maybe this is my punishment.'

'You did nothing to deserve this, Joanna, but it's a valuable lesson and you will recover in time. Thank you for telling me.'

'You're not angry at me, Alice, for ... you know, with the prince?'

'Only disappointed for you, Joanna, and sorry for you.'

CHAPTER NINE

The court of Poitiers bid a relieved farewell to summer's heat, and Prince Henry was replaced by his solid younger brother, Richard, who did not have his brother's angelic looks. Colder weather meant the retreat of many courtiers back to their own castles to prepare for winter, and Eleanor's court enjoyed a period of much needed calm and reflection.

Eleanor became gay again in the presence of her favourite son, and the absence of Henry and Bertran encouraged Joanna's recovery.

The week before Christmas, Eleanor, Marie and Richard prepared to leave for Paris, where they would meet King Henry at King Louis' court to discuss their children's inheritance. Eleanor's attending ladies — including Alice and Joanna — were kept busy preparing her furs, jewels, undergarments, cosmetics and perfumes for the trip. Eleanor would require a different gown every evening at banquet, as well as twelve different furs to match. As well as that she would need her winter hawking camouflage, her headdresses and veils, and thirty different pairs of footwear.

Alice and Joanna were with the other attending ladies in the Tower. They fussed around Eleanor's wardrobe in the chamber which let in the most winter sunshine. Many of Eleanor's intimate items were spread out on the wide oak table. Alice was sitting alone, as usual, stitching gold embroidery onto one of Eleanor's hems, while Joanna was sorting Eleanor's ear jewels at the table with Lady Rosemary. These two had become friends of sorts, but Alice observed they often bickered. Some natural rivalry existed between them, and it seemed that

Bertran had switched his attentions from Joanna to Rosemary of late. Rosemary had looked peaky with envy when she found out that Eleanor had invited Alice and Joanna to join at Chinon for Christmas.

Joanna was trying to console her. 'Think of what a peaceful time you shall have when we are all hard at work.'

'I do not wish for peace,' Rosemary complained. 'I want jolly times and dancing, same as you!'

'Perhaps you should ask the queen to take you along, then,' Joanna suggested. 'Maybe it was just an oversight? Nobody paints the charcoal on her eyes as well as you.'

'Oh, that's not it,' said Rosemary, bitterly. 'King Henry showed a marked liking for me when I was at his court in England. I did not allow him to touch me, unlike the other ladies. I was always faithful to Her. But I believe it caused Eleanor pain to see him chase after me. That is why she does not want me to join them at Chinon for Christmas. I must be punished for my beauty and spend a lonely Christmas.'

'Do you think Eleanor would worry about that now? I mean, after so much time has passed?' Joanna asked.

'I don't see any other reason why she would leave me behind, do you?' Rosemary snapped.

'Well, perhaps she does not have room for everyone?'

'At Chinon?' Rosemary exclaimed. 'Chinon is huge.'

The other ladies agreed.

'Hold your tongues, Eleanor is coming,' Alice cautioned. Rosemary threw her eyes to the heavens.

Eleanor swept into the room in a whirl of loveliness. Her face and eyes had captured the fresh air of her morning walk. 'Well, ladies? How are we getting on with the preparations?'

'We are getting on nicely, my lady,' Alice replied. 'Would you check this fur, to see if it needs to be replaced? It is perhaps a little old.'

'I'll ask Richard to check everything this afternoon,' Eleanor said, eyes twinkling. 'Please leave all my things spread out just like that on the table until he comes. I must leave you again, I have so much to prepare!' She turned back. 'Joanna, I almost forgot. I've sent for my own hairdresser to cut your hair this afternoon in your chamber. Alice, you may accompany her.'

'That is so unfair!' said Rosemary, after Eleanor had gone. 'You are to be favoured with a new haircut, as well as keeping Christmas at Chinon!'

Alice interceded kindly on Joanna's part. 'She needs to have her hair cut nicely, while yours could not be any lovelier.'

That pleased Rosemary enough to keep her quiet, and she flicked back her long yellow locks proudly. Joanna's hair was growing back, but it was uneven.

'There is no need for you to accompany me, Alice,' Joanna said. 'I would be happier to go alone.'

'Very well,' said Alice, 'I have all this stitching to finish.'

They had developed a new understanding that Joanna should be treated as a grownup in certain matters, and Alice never attempted to advise her on her wardrobe or appearance now.

When Alice thought sufficient time had lapsed for Joanna's hair to be dressed, she slipped out, leaving the chattering ladies behind. She knocked gently on their chamber door.

'Come in.'

Joanna was sitting at the glass, anxiously smoothing her hands over her new pageboy cut.

'It suits you wonderfully!' Alice said. 'Are you happy with it?'

Joanna looked relieved, but assumed a complacent air. 'I do not really mind it,' she said, breezily. 'I suppose it looks better.'

'Yes, and it is such a pretty colour,' Alice encouraged. 'It frames your lovely face.'

Joanna looked happier. 'I've laid my new dresses on the bed, if you'd like to see? I think they will suit my new hair well.'

All the dresses were cut to emphasize Joanna's figure. She had chosen natural colours to cleverly simulate the nude form. They were not openly provocative, but subtly so. The matching furs were dyed blood-red. Alice was disappointed; she'd hoped that by trusting Joanna and allowing her more freedom, she would prove less rebellious. She caught Joanna observing her reaction to the clothing in the glass. With a little shock, she saw the small, ironic smile playing on her lips. Was Joanna consciously rebelling against her, against her conservatism?

'How do you like them, Alice?' Joanna's tone was mocking.

'They are not really to my taste, as you know,' Alice answered, coldly. 'I do not find this flaxen colour flattering at all and the furs are most sensual, not at all suitable for a maid.'

Joanna laughed lightly. 'Have you had any new dresses made up, Alice?'

'No, my old ones are sufficient,' Alice replied, curtly.

'So, it will be the customary black, I suppose? Would you not try Mama's burgundy cloak for a change?' Joanna suggested, her tone kinder.

'Absolutely not!' Alice snapped, missing her tone. 'Do you intend me to make an exhibition of myself?'

'No!' Joanna replied, defensively. 'Why should you not wear something festive, like everyone else? Why should you not dress up? What are you so afraid of?'

'I am not afraid,' said Alice, composing herself. 'I am simply not worth noticing. It would be ridiculous to hang anything decorative off me. I have forsaken outward beauty for riches of the soul.'

'You sound like a martyr,' said Joanna, dryly.

'Do not speak to me like that,' Alice warned. 'Show some respect for your elders.'

'Very well,' said Joanna. 'I'm sorry if I caused you offence, I only wanted to help. I see that I was wrong. I must be very greedy to desire both inward *and* outward beauty!'

Alice sighed.

'Do you think Lady Rosemary is very pretty?' Joanna asked, suddenly.

'She is fair and chaste,' Alice replied, 'but she forgets her manners sometimes, like someone else I know.'

Joanna swung around and looked Alice boldly in the eye. 'She is chaste all right; she told me she has not let any man touch her. I suspect she is frigid, for it is unnatural not to desire a man's touch.'

'That's enough, Joanna.'

Alice suspected that Joanna was making comment on her status as an old maid, as well as making a nasty dig at her rival.

CHAPTER TEN

Packed into an ox cart, Alice and Joanna endured a bumpy, sleepless journey through the night. The cart spilled them out before a gaping, black river which made curious sucking sounds like a babe at the teat. They waited until first light for the boat that would take them upriver to Chinon. The men-at-arms who had accompanied them turned back for Poitiers.

Mysterious in his hooded cloak, the boatman threw their carpet bags aboard before helping them on and showing them to a nest of wool among the logs where they could bunk down. As light broke, they slept through the last cries of bullfrogs desperate for a mate; they even slept through the horns of bigger boats as the river expanded and grew busy, like a pot-bellied man of influence.

Only when the boat seized and lurched violently did they wake. Alice stumbled up to the front and discovered they had passed through the Chinon dam. When the castle came into view, its vastness gave Joanna a queer feeling; they'd be utterly lost here, she feared.

Chinon was a maze of tiny, cobbled streets reaching out from the imposing castle's defences like the roots of an ancient tree. Mist from the river shrouded it in an eerie morning haze.

Alice and Joanna stood small and forlorn with their carpet bags. They waited for an age, but no men-at-arms came to meet them. It must have been an oversight on Eleanor's part, so they decided to make their own way to the castle.

The streets were far dirtier and noisier than Poitiers, but they had a vital energy and plenty for their eyes and ears to feast on. Yeoman's stalls heaved with country produce and friars unashamedly extended their begging bowls to passers-by, while young prostitutes arched their taut little bodies against the wall like stealthy cats. When the bell struck nine, the streets were alive with tanners, weavers, bakers, blacksmiths, candle makers, perfume sellers, dyers, spice and silk merchants, and pipe and instrument makers.

Dusty and thirsty, Alice and Joanna decided to stop at a small shop for refreshment. The place fell quiet as they walked up to a man in dusty robes. He brought them barley and a pot of boiled water, which he placed over a flame. He placed the barley into the water, stirring slowly, before straining it into two tumblers and adding spices. He did all this without looking at the two ladies; he didn't care who his customers were, so long as they could pay.

'We could be commoners,' whispered Joanna, excitedly. 'Perhaps we should roam around for a while in disguise?'

'Certainly not! Our clothes are dusty enough,' grumbled Alice. 'You know it's not safe.'

They laboured up the steep, cobbled path and were stopped by guards at the castle gates.

'We are attending ladies to the Duchess of Poitiers, Queen of England,' Alice explained, showing the guards Eleanor's seal. They were asked to wait while a messenger was dispatched. Moments later, Marie appeared and rushed forward to greet them.

'We did not expect you on the early ferry,' she explained. 'We thought you were coming later, otherwise we would never have left you unattended!'

'Oh, it doesn't matter,' said Joanna. 'It was fun to go about the place unattended.'

'What is your first impression of Chinon?' Marie asked.

'I like it,' said Joanna instantly.

'It's dirty and overcrowded,' Alice said.

Marie laughed. 'You'll get used to it,' she said. 'It's not so bad and there's lots here to entertain. It's safer than it seems. Though —' she lowered her voice — 'you'll find it rather coarse compared with my mother's court. Let me take you straight to our chambers. Here at Chinon, all the attending ladies stay in my mother's bedchamber. Don't worry, there is plenty of space for everyone. You can unpack and settle in and then join us for refreshments. It's lovely to see you!'

Alice and Joanna followed Marie through an enormous archway and up a turret stairwell that opened onto a stone chamber as big as a chapel. They recognized the furs and headdresses that they'd helped to pack. Curtains hanging between the ladies' cots and Eleanor's heavy mahogany bed lent a touch of warmth, but the air was cold, despite the hearty fire in the grate. Some other ladies were sitting about, either idly or with needlework. Marie greeted them with a nod, before drawing a curtain between them.

'There, now, you will have some privacy while you change,' she said.

'Where shall we find you after?' asked Alice.

'Just at the bottom of the stairwell, there is a door inside the archway. That's where we ladies take our refreshments during the day. Of course, at night we all gather in one of the banqueting halls.'

'One of the banqueting halls?' Joanna queried.

'There are three!' Marie said. 'There are so many musicians and entertainers and just as many courtiers, so the different halls are required to accommodate everyone. Sometimes male and female courtiers are even separated into different halls. Especially during the Christmas season, when the royal family is gathered together.'

Alice asked the ladies where to wash and they pointed to a crude pipe with running water where she could fill her jug. She splashed her face at the ceramic basin, but could not bear to wash in the cold. They changed into woollen dresses and tied short velvet capes around their shoulders. To Alice's amusement, Joanna slipped on the long, thin shoes with curled toes, currently fashionable. She sat at Eleanor's glass and painted a dramatic charcoal rim around her eyes. She then brushed her lids with crushed ochre and gold leaf, making her eyes shine like sapphires. Alice wondered when she'd learnt to use cosmetics. She watched Joanna carefully tying a black velvet bow around her smooth new hair, her youthful form graceful as a dancer's. They'd been there only a short while, yet Joanna's things were already strewn all over the place.

'Do try to keep your things together,' said Alice irritably.

Alice and Joanna hesitated a moment at the day-chamber door, neither of them wanting to enter first.

'Oh, very well!' Joanna said, pushing open the door.

They found themselves in another dreary stone building with heavy wooden vaulting overhead. The floor was strewn with straw and the tables were laden with white linen and fat candles to make up for the lack of windows providing natural light. Marie spotted them and stood up in her place. She was sitting with some ladies, who left after they'd been introduced.

'I'm afraid I must go shortly, too,' Marie apologised. 'We are preparing the entertainment for tonight's banquet. King Henry and Richard are out hunting and shan't return till after dark. Don't be alarmed, Alice!' Marie smiled. 'Henry only attends the evening banquets, and then he is much preoccupied. You'll find my mother in excellent spirits. She has much to celebrate. My father took her part in persuading Henry to give Aquitaine to Richard. I'm happy, for Richard is a splendid fellow and would make a much better Duke than young Henry. Richard is extremely grateful to my father for his intervention.'

'Oh, that is marvellous news!' said Joanna, relieved. Alice too was all smiles. They'd have hated Henry to be Duke of Poitiers.

'It makes much more sense,' said Marie, 'for how could young Henry have ruled it as well as the other kingdoms he is to inherit? He'd have ruled from England, but then the barons would've become disgruntled, as they did before my mother returned. Henry does not even speak their language as Richard does; he does not understand their culture.'

Alice had a queer, sinking sensation. So, Marie had found in Richard the brother she had hoped to find in young Henry. Alice hoped she would not be spending all her time with him and neglecting her.

The great hall was bare and ugly by day, but by night it was transformed. Flames rose up like magic snakes licking the air, and exotic lanterns shed enchanting stars and shapes around the walls. Fragrant lily-shaped candles floated in the ancient aqueducts, which had been filled with wine instead of water. All Eleanor's work, of course; Alice had helped to cut the shapes out of the lanterns.

Alice and Joanna sat just a few rows back from Eleanor and King Henry, surrounded by other ladies. Joanna had changed into one of her new dresses, a figure-hugging, skin- coloured velvet, with the bodice cut low and two miniscule strips for sleeves. Her footwear mimicked Eleanor's own bright, violet slippers with curled up toes. With her short hair and small frame, she looked neither girl nor boy, but fairy or elfin.

'Did you see the king's party returning from the hunt?' whispered Joanna. 'Didn't they look like savages in their rough robes? The king is such a stout man, it's a wonder his horse doesn't collapse under him!'

The king and queen made a contrasting pair; Eleanor, in her ivory gown with jewels sparkling in her auburn hair and Henry, flame-cheeked and dressed like a peasant in a coarse, woollen tunic. Like day and night when they stood together, they exchanged no intimate looks or touches, but gazed ahead of them like statues. They were the only male and female sitting together in the hall.

'There is more separation between the sexes here than at Poitiers,' Joanna observed.

'Indeed,' said Alice, 'I think it is more comfortable, don't you?'

'I do not,' said Joanna, decidedly. 'Men and women should treat each other as equals, and separation hardly encourages easy relations. At least the musicians all go around together regardless,' she added. 'They have to, for practice.'

'For practice?'

'Musically speaking, Alice! I met some nice musicians today I hope to befriend. I am to sing with them on Christmas Eve. We'll be practising hard every day.'

'That's nice,' said Alice, glad that Joanna had regained her desire to perform after her dreadful ordeal.

A great feast of roast crane and spiced winter roots was served with jugs of wine. Heralds blew trumpets between the courses and marshals waved wands between the juggling, tumbling and clowning acts on stage.

'I do hope the music is better than these clowns!' sighed Alice.

Joanna laughed. 'Don't worry,' she said, 'the music will be much better.'

'Shall we go to bed?' suggested Alice once they had eaten. 'We've had a long day.'

'I'm not a bit tired,' said Joanna, gaily. 'I think I'll stay a bit longer.'

Alice wished Joanna would attend her, both for company and safety, but she was trying to treat her as an adult. 'Of course,' she said, quickly, 'come to bed whenever you please.'

The next morning, all the ladies rose early and the bedchamber was a hive of activity with the maids all bustling about carrying heavy gowns and porcelain combs, cosmetics and bedpans. The shutters were thrown open on the narrow, glassless windows and a fire was lit.

Every year on the sixth day before Christmas, the ladies of Chinon gathered for a lunch dressed all in white, to symbolize purity. Alice and Joanna, along with Eleanor's other maids, helped the queen into a snow leopard fur and attached a delicate silk-spun veil over her matching fur skullcap with a cluster of pearls. With their fingertips, they massaged rose paste into her pale cheeks to make them dewy and dabbed her pulses with ambergris.

Carrying a silver staff capped with a diamond star, Eleanor led them all downstairs. The tables had been laid with frosted buns, ices and jellies and the day room had been beautifully decorated, with white and pink spindle in tall glasses and silk webs hanging from the ceiling. All the attending ladies were required to wear white, so even Alice had borrowed a white shift and cloak to replace the steadfast black, much to Joanna's amusement. At midday, bowls of raspberries were carried in, followed by a fountain of hot, white chocolate. Eleanor was presented with a large, glass globe containing an effervescent liquid. She looked quizzically at her ladies, but they were as surprised as she.

'A gift from king Henry,' the messenger explained.

'Oh!' Eleanor peered at the little mound of ice inside the globe. 'Sparkling wine chilled with mountain snow! That is the trouble with Henry,' she confided. 'He can be impossibly charming!' She shared the wine out into silver thimbles.

Alice and Joanna listened quietly as the conversation turned to serious matters.

'This business with Thomas Becket must be resolved,' Eleanor said to Marie. 'He and Henry have had a dreadful falling out and Becket has left his seat and moved abroad. It is intolerable not to have the Archbishop of Canterbury in his seat! Really, they are both so stubborn, I cannot see how it will be resolved peacefully. It has already caused serious impediments to Church and State. It is foolish of Henry to let the situation continue. Young Henry's education was ceased because of it and now, as you know, my husband has promised Louis that Marguerite will be crowned with young Henry, but the Archbishop of Canterbury — none other than Thomas Becket — must preside over the ceremony! If Louis' daughter is not crowned, Richard's position as future Duke may be jeopardized.'

Her speech was interrupted by Richard's entrance. He was dressed in a splendid white tunic with silver brocade sleeves and buttons.

'I hope you don't mind my intruding, ladies,' he said. 'I shall only stay a moment. Mama.' He kissed Eleanor's hand.

'You may stay as long as you like, Richard; you are like an honorary lady!' Eleanor said, laughing.

After admiring their costumes, Richard sat down.

'I was just speaking of this tiresome business between Henry and Thomas Becket,' Eleanor said. 'I think it very foolish of my husband not to resolve it at once. It has caused many problems already and will continue to do so. It is damaging Henry's popularity and costing the Crown, for donations are being withheld in protest. You should persuade him, Richard, to seek a reconciliation with Becket. The Crown at odds with the Church is like a head at odds with its body; one cannot function without the other.'

'And yet I fear my father would happily remove Becket's head,' joked Richard.

'It's not funny, Richard, it's sad; they used to be such close friends. I cannot even recall what they are quarrelling over, can you?'

'It is a minor matter,' said Richard, 'that could be resolved easily, but it is really about power, rather than religion.'

'How did it all start, Richard?' asked Marie.

'Henry doesn't agree with clerics being tried for crimes in a separate court to lay people. Clerics have — quite literally — been getting away with murder for years, and Henry wants to put a stop to that. As part of his policy of reform, he has drawn up a new law, The Constitution of Clarendon, to the effect that clerics be tried for crimes the same as lay people. Becket agreed to sign it, but then he changed his mind and fled across the channel at the last moment. The law does not hold unless the archbishop signs.'

'Why does Henry insist on changing age-old laws, anyway, upsetting the balance?' Eleanor sighed. 'He takes it on himself to change the constitution, but he doesn't consider the consequences. Your brother's coronation and your future position as Duke both depend on this quarrel ending. If your brother is not crowned, he would certainly seek the Duchy as compensation. If Louis' daughter, Marguerite is not crowned, it will upset Louis and he may withdraw his offers to both you and Geoffrey. Do you see, Richard, how this affects us?'

'I do, Mama,' said Richard, grimly. He rose and paced about the room. His easy-going manner had fled and been replaced by a moody restlessness. It was the same alteration Alice had observed in Eleanor whenever Henry thwarted her plans. Richard and Eleanor bore the same expression now, like a vicious snow leopard and her hungry cub.

Alice was surprised to find herself feeling sorry for King Henry. It seemed reasonable for him to want clerics to be tried for crimes the same as lay people. Eleanor and Richard were clearly united in their dislike of the king, but from what Alice had observed, Henry doted on his children and indulged Eleanor. Before coming to Chinon, she'd heard only terrible things about his lechery, infidelities and raging fits of temper, but she'd seen there was another side to him that was thoughtful and intelligent. Why else would Eleanor have fallen in love with him? But she would never breathe a word in Henry's favour — even to Joanna — out of loyalty to Eleanor.

That night, a sea-themed banquet was prepared. The food had been cast into fantastical shapes. Swordfish brandished overhead, all shimmering pinks and silvers in the candlelight, gold platters laid with pink starfish made from river trout were passed down tables and jellies, cleverly shaped as jellyfish, were wobbling in glass bowls.

Eleanor made her entrance dressed as a mermaid, with Alice and three others carrying her jewelled tail. Henry took his place in a magnificent, pea-green robe. With his crown of seaweed and golden staff, he looked every inch the sea-king.

Joanna stood out among the musicians in an emerald dress, with a thin crown of emeralds in her hair and an exquisite pair of long, embroidered slippers. Her singing was pure and sweet and her movements light and free.

Alice had saved a seat in the hopes her niece would join her afterwards, but Joanna disappeared into the crowd. At midnight, Alice decided to take herself off to bed. Just as she was about to climb the stairwell, she heard Joanna's laugh coming from the day room. She creaked the door open cautiously and peered inside. Joanna was nestled in a chair, chatting with a fellow so skinny, with such long hair, she almost took him for a girl. She recognized him as one of the musicians. The others were sitting around, harmlessly drinking barley water or smoking pipes. Alice was afraid it was improper for Joanna to be talking so freely with a boy, but she left again silently. She would ask Marie's advice tomorrow; it would give her a good excuse to seek her out.

CHAPTER ELEVEN

Alice, her new skirt swishing, rushed out after Marie the next morning. She'd left Joanna sleeping, hoping to slip back before she woke. They would all need to attend to Eleanor shortly, as it was Christmas day and her costume would be elaborate.

'Alice.' Marie turned and noticed her serious face. 'Is everything all right?'

A lady passing on her way to breakfast slowed to listen in.

'Oh, yes, everything is well.' Alice dared not speak openly in company. 'I just wanted to walk with you.'

'Of course, how nice,' said Marie. 'We've not had much time to chat here, have we? I'm sorry I've been so busy.'

'Oh, I understand, I've been very much occupied myself.' Alice did not want Marie to think her needy.

'I'm sure my mother is keeping you occupied,' smiled Marie, 'but I am glad to have you to myself a little while.'

The warm words melted Alice's cool. 'Oh, so am I!' she exclaimed. 'Actually, there is something I wanted to ask you about.' The other lady had passed on.

'Don't tell me,' said Marie, 'does it concern Joanna?'

'How did you guess?' Alice asked.

'With you it is always about Joanna,' said Marie. 'You know my opinion and it remains unchanged; I think you should let Joanna fight her own battles.'

'Yes, you are right,' said Alice, quickly, 'but this is just a little thing I wanted your advice on. You know —' she hesitated — 'you have more experience of men than I do.'

'Go on, I am listening,' said Marie, curious now.

They stopped in an archway, drawing their cloaks close against the biting breeze. Marie's linen veil was loose and flapping, pale blue against her sallow skin. A strand of her dark hair whipped around her face. Alice's headdress was black and stiff as a coffin in unfair contrast to her pallor. Marie's warm brown eyes looked eagerly into hers. Alice was unsure how to begin. Embarrassed, she glanced down at the bundle of scores in Marie's hand. 'Are you meeting with the musicians?' she asked.

'First thing, though many of them are probably still in bed!'

'Joanna is still sleeping. She's been up till after midnight every night. Last night, as I was going to bed, I heard laughter from the day room and peeked in. The musicians were there, and Joanna was sitting cosily with one of them — a boy.'

'Ah,' said Marie, 'I see. And you're worried about the boy?'

'Well, yes,' Alice admitted. 'I don't know it it's seemly for Joanna to go around with him.'

Marie shifted. 'Seemly? Why on earth would it not be seemly?'

Alice felt foolish. 'I don't know the rules, and then there is the matter of Joanna's reputation, which is already damaged, as you know. Eleanor did say she'd need to prove herself before it would blow over.'

'I see.' Marie considered. 'I don't like the separation between the sexes here at Chinon; in fact, I believe it fosters perversity. Have you noticed how many prostitutes there are? At least Joanna and Jean are open in their friendship. I think that's good.'

'You know him? Jean?'

'I've noticed they are friends, nothing more. They are the youngest of the group, so it's natural they should pair themselves off. I suppose you feel left out?' Marie patted Alice's arm.

'No, certainly not,' said Alice, defensively. 'I'm relieved it's innocent. I didn't know. Joanna and I have not spoken about him… I'll not worry now.'

'Jean is sweet and harmless,' Marie assured Alice. 'If anything, Joanna would be more likely to lead him astray.'

Alice didn't return her smile.

'I'm jesting, come on! Don't worry, Alice. But let's go in, it's freezing.'

'You go on,' Alice said. 'I must return to the bedchamber to assist Eleanor's dressing.'

'You look miserable,' said Marie. 'Why don't you come with me? You can meet Jean yourself. And the hall's much warmer than the bedchamber!'

'Oh, no, I'd better not…'

'Come, Alice, my mother can spare you for an hour or so. Take a little time for yourself for a change.'

'Well, all right, I suppose I could,' Alice said, cheering up.

Marie linked her arm. She was so wholesome — unlike her elusive mother — and Alice took pleasure in her openness, wishing she was less uptight herself. Happy for her hand to be crushed into Marie's generous arm, she listened as Marie spoke of Eleanor and Richard.

Alice sat quietly in the background as the musicians practised. When Joanna entered, she saw Alice but she didn't even nod. Alice was worried she'd think she was spying on her. After a while, Marie joined her. 'So,' she whispered, 'are you satisfied with Jean?'

'You are right,' Alice said, 'he's innocuous.' Inwardly she chastised herself for betraying how preoccupied she still was with Joanna. She was afraid Marie would think her mind unclean, for jumping to conclusions. 'He seems well-mannered,' she commented.

'He's the youngest son of a Viscount hereabouts with no land to inherit, so he's turned to music, happily for us. Now — ' Marie changed the subject — 'speaking of inheritance, Richard was to speak with his father this morning concerning this business with Thomas Becket. If all goes smoothly, my mother will have her vassals swear fealty to him on his thirteenth birthday. Imagine my brother as Duke, Alice, wouldn't he be marvellous?'

'Yes!' Alice agreed, though she feared the time and energy Marie would devote to him and take from her. She felt the pain of loss already in her chest, like it was caving in.

Marie did not notice her sudden shortness of breath. 'I must go,' she said, rising suddenly, 'and seek him out at once! I almost forgot, Richard and I are to greet the first guests in the mead hall this afternoon. I shall see you there!'

With so many ladies to fuss over her, Eleanor hadn't noticed Alice's absence. Her Christmas gown was a heavy, scarlet velvet lined with weasel fur and her headdress was tied with a bright gold circlet.

'My lady, you look wonderful,' Alice declared.

'I do not care for Christmas day,' Eleanor sighed. 'All that ritual over which I must preside. I'd prefer to tear this headdress off and run freely through the grounds. I may do just that tomorrow!' She smiled. 'Well, at least tomorrow I may go hawking to my heart's content. Ladies, let's go and greet our guests!'

They attended her up the narrow stairwell to the mead hall above the banqueting hall. The massive fireplace acted as conduit to the winds groaning and keening through the walls. The ladies made pleasant conversation as they flitted about with the mead jugs, but Alice served silently and didn't mingle. *Tomorrow,* she thought, *I'll reward myself with a quiet day alone.*

By evening, many were already sleeping off their drunkenness. Alice hung about as Joanna changed into her evening dress.

'You sang prettily,' said Alice.

'I think you were the only one sober enough to hear!'

Alice blinked at Joanna's costume. It was a tactile mink, slinky as silk, the same creamy colour as her skin. She had tied a string of amethysts round her throat. 'I've never seen those on you,' Alice said as she touched them.

'I've never worn them before,' Joanna said. 'They were Mama's favourite.'

Alice wondered why she'd chosen this night to wear them. 'They suit you well,' she said. 'No princess could look finer. You could pass for Eleanor's daughter! I shall be proud to be seen with you.'

'Well, Eleanor is not my mother, and I am not a princess,' Joanna declared, 'only a count's daughter, unfortunately.'

'You do look up to Eleanor, don't you?'

'Of course,' Joanna replied, 'we all look up to her.'

'But you look up to her like a mother,' Alice persisted, missing Joanna's defensive tone.

Joanna's lips curled down. 'She's not my mother! I have no mother! You make me sound like a sycophant. I don't believe I look up to Eleanor any more than you look up to Princess Marie!'

Alice was startled. 'What do you mean, dear?' she asked. 'Marie and I are friends...'

'I only mean, dear Alice, that perhaps I take more after you than you think. We both of us look up to royalty — the way you're always watching Marie?'

A deep frown creased Alice's forehead. 'I'm not always watching her,' she said, quietly.

'I meant nothing by it, Alice. Why shouldn't we admire them? Gives us something to aspire to…'

'Quiet, child,' said Alice. 'That's enough now.'

Joanna shrugged and walked out.

Alice drew the curtains around their bed, curling up for warmth. She'd not go down for evening banquet. Nobody would miss her, nobody would care. Joanna's words had opened a black hole of fear in her. Confronted with her own, grasping nature, she felt sick with self-loathing. She must look foolish to others, running after Marie, hungry for titbits of affection from the princess.

CHAPTER TWELVE

Alice woke early and extracted herself from Joanna. Voices speaking urgently caused her to sit up and listen. She heard 'Richard' and 'Henry' uttered most and guessed that something important must have happened the night before. She hesitated to rise, worried in case she might intrude. She coughed, making a little racket so they'd be warned. Joanna stirred, casting her eyes about in confusion.

'Shhh.' Alice held a finger to her lips. 'Listen.'

'You know how drunk he gets.' It was Marie's voice. 'He didn't mean those things. You'll see, today he'll be sorry.'

'But every year it's the same,' argued Eleanor. 'He flies into a rage and then demands to be forgiven. I don't know why I agreed to keep Christmas with him. I'll certainly not dine with him today.'

'No one would blame you,' said Marie.

'Ladies!' Eleanor called. 'Gather round me, please.'

They all went to attend their queen.

Still in her scarlet gown and pale with lack of sleep, Eleanor was holding Marie's hand. Alice's heart flushed with sympathy.

'Has something happened, Eleanor?' Joanna asked, alarmed. 'Are you unwell?'

'Dear Joanna, no, don't worry. Henry flew into one of his rages last night and insulted Richard and I in front of our courtiers. Accused us of plotting against him and siding with Thomas Becket. He was writhing around on the floor, had to be restrained and dragged off to bed. It's frightening when he takes one of his fits...'

'Did he hurt you?' Joanna was shocked.

'He's never laid a hand on me — or any of his children — but his brutal words have as much force as a thousand blows,' Eleanor said, wearily. 'Poor Richard bore the brunt of it, and for that I am sorry.'

They helped Eleanor out of her dress, removed her cosmetics with rose water and applied ointment to her tired skin and eyes. She lay down to rest, still clutching Marie's hand.

'Tomorrow we'll go hawking,' said Joanna, 'then none of this will seem important.'

Eleanor smiled faintly and nodded. As she slept, the ladies talked among themselves.

'Heed my words,' said a well-seasoned lady, 'he'll crawl back to her on hands and knees, begging for forgiveness. He always does!'

'I'm not so sure,' said an elegant lady with defined cheekbones, from the English court. 'This quarrel with Becket runs so deep with him, he considers it treason if anyone interferes.'

'Yes, that's true,' said the first. 'But he'll be sorry just the same. He values his family above all else, despite appearances.'

'I hope you're right.'

'Do you think Eleanor will be all right?' asked Joanna, concerned.

'Oh, certainly, my dear, you mustn't worry. She's used to his rages. She was just upset that Richard had to bear the brunt of it.'

'Why are husbands so vicious?' asked Joanna, angrily.

The other ladies smiled grimly.

'They are not all vicious,' said the older lady. 'Some of them are kind and considerate.'

'Well, none that I know of,' argued Joanna.

The sound of clattering hooves drove them out into the courtyard. The king's men were embarking on a hunt, but the king was not among them.

'Where's the king?' one of the ladies asked.

'The king is in the chapel, praying for forgiveness of his sins.' That was good news for Eleanor.

The sky was thickly laden with snow clouds and the paths were treacherous with ice, so Alice and Joanna returned indoors to warm themselves before the fire. After noon, the door flung open and Richard entered with purpose.

'Good afternoon, ladies,' he said. 'Has my mother risen yet?'

'The queen is still asleep,' Alice said. 'Take a cushion and join us.'

He sprawled his long legs out before the fire, regaling them with details of the fight with King Henry. Richard's story was interrupted by a message for Joanna. A young man was waiting for her outside.

'Please ask him to come back later,' said Joanna, irritably. 'Or tomorrow.'

Alice noticed that her niece's jaw had clenched in irritation. She guessed Jean and Joanna had been in an argument. Surely that's why Joanna had come to bed so early? She pressed Joanna's hand.

'That's right,' Alice said, 'we'd better stay here. Eleanor will need her ladies when she wakes.'

'We are leaving early,' Marie informed them when she and Eleanor joined them round the fire. 'We're to return to Poitiers in the morning. It's too late to embark on a journey; darkness is already blotting out the day.'

'Mama, are you sure that's wise?' asked Richard, concerned.

'Yes, my dear Richard,' Eleanor said. 'It's the best course for us. I've already dispatched the message to Henry. There is no point in prolonging the misery.'

Alice and Joanna were delighted; they longed to return to Poitiers, though some of the ladies worried that Henry would take offense.

'Forgive us,' one of them said, 'but don't you need the king's permission to leave early?'

Marie shot a worried glance at Eleanor. Alice observed the dark circles under Marie's eyes and tried to catch her eye in sympathy, but she was too absorbed in her mother.

'This is a family affair,' Eleanor said, 'not a public one. I don't believe we need to obtain Henry's permission to leave a little early. We've performed our festive duties, kept up our side of things. It's Henry who has let us down.'

'It cannot matter much if we leave a few days early,' Richard decided, 'and I'm eager to return to Poitiers. I'm sick of the conditions here. I never want to see — or smell — another farting clown! Although, Mama, it's unlikely that father will ask Becket to preside over my brother's coronation now, and if Henry isn't crowned, I'll not be made duke...'

'You shall be made duke, Richard, don't fear,' Eleanor said. 'I mean for you to have Aquitaine — with or without Henry's blessing! Even if it means getting King Louis' backing by covert means.'

A word blew through Alice: *treason*. She barely dared to think of it.

Marie looked at Eleanor, utterly alarmed. 'Mother, come, let's eat something.'

'Ah, yes,' said Eleanor, 'I'm ravenous. Ladies, come with us and take a glass of ale.'

The messenger returned with a letter from Henry to say that he was sorry and begged their forgiveness. He invited Eleanor and Richard to dine alone with him that evening. Without the queen's daughter, he specified. Marie hung her head. As Louis' daughter, Henry didn't trust her. Eleanor and Richard exchanged a look of triumph.

'This is good,' Eleanor said. 'Tell Henry we shall come.'

'You don't mind leaving your new friends?' Alice asked Joanna, as they packed.

'Oh, no,' Joanna declared, 'it's so vast and tiresome here. Honestly, I'm relieved to be leaving. Thank God we don't live here, Alice. It's so dark and strange!'

'Well, it's winter now,' said Alice. 'I'm sure it's a happier place in summer. I know what you mean, though. Our castle at Poitiers is much more comfortable.'

'I can't believe this is Henry's favourite estate... Imagine how dreary his English court must be if he prefers it here! No wonder Eleanor wanted to return to Poitiers. I wonder what he wants to speak to them about. I hope she tells us!'

Alice pitied Marie; Eleanor had rushed off without giving her any words of consolation. As soon as Joanna had left to bid farewell to Jean and the other musicians, Alice went to Marie. She found her undressing and, embarrassed, turned away.

'My apologies, I wanted only to extend my sympathies... It can wait,' Alice muttered, retreating.

'Come back, Alice!' Marie called after her. 'I'm perfectly respectable like this, among friends. I'm sure my shift is much the same as yours!'

Marie's pretty embroidered undergarment was nothing like Alice's plain one. *Blue is her colour*, Alice noticed. *Makes her dark skin glow.*

'I thought you were marvellous with Eleanor this morning,' Alice gushed. 'You bring her such comfort, truly. It was a shame you weren't included in the king's invitation this evening. It must have hurt you deeply.'

Marie's eyes twinkled warmly. 'Alice, you worry too much about the feelings of others,' she declared. 'I was not in the least offended. On the contrary, had I been invited, I should have been forced to think of some elaborate excuse not to attend!'

Alice was puzzled.

'It would have placed me in a compromised position regarding my father, King Louis.' Marie spoke as if reminding Alice of something she must already know.

'Forgive me.' Alice was glad of the darkness hiding her blushes. 'I had not thought of that.'

Marie's brow furrowed suddenly. 'I would be compromised by witnessing whatever agreement Mother and Henry arrive at. May I confide fully in you, Alice?'

'Please,' Alice urged, 'confide in me, I wish for nothing more.' She placed her thin, cold hand over Marie's soft, warm one.

'Thank you, my dear,' Marie said. 'I'm grateful for your friendship.'

Alice's heart fluttered with pleasure and her chest expanded with warmth.

'You see, my father has an agenda. He has ostensibly taken my mother and Richard's part regarding Aquitaine, but the matter is not that simple. The problem of Thomas Becket is by no means disposable, and neither are the terms of inheritance clear among the brothers. Up till now, young Henry meant to inherit both his father's kingdom and Aquitaine. But who will crown him? Not the Archbishop of Canterbury, Thomas Becket. Who do you think young Henry will blame if he's not crowned? His father, of course. Who will Richard blame if he doesn't inherit Aquitaine? Don't you see, Alice? Louis is fostering dissension within the ranks. It is his agenda to cause strife between the brothers and their father. His policy is to divide and conquer. By weakening their stronghold, he strengthens his own.'

'I see,' said Alice. 'I must admit I was surprised when I heard of Louis' magnanimous diplomacy. Does Eleanor not see Louis' agenda? She's so clever, I find it had to believe she doesn't see...'

'Yes, of course she sees!' said Marie. 'But Louis is manipulating her. All my mother cares about is holding onto Aquitaine for Richard. My father hasn't created the division; the discord was already there.'

'What about King Henry?' questioned Alice. 'Surely he sees what's under his very nose?'

'I don't know,' Marie sighed. 'I don't know the king well enough to say. That's why I was glad not to be included in his invitation. I don't want to be privy to anything he might say that would place me in a compromised position with my father. That is my agenda. To carry on peacefully with my poetic endeavours.'

They heard footsteps on the stairs and held their breaths. It was just Joanna. She stopped abruptly before them, startled at the sight of Marie in her undershift. Her eyes fell on their hands, still clasped together. Alice withdrew hers furtively.

'Has Eleanor returned?' Joanna asked.

'Not yet,' said Alice. 'We must be patient. Come, let's finish packing.'

Joanna rubbed her tired eyes as Alice fussed around her.

'Did you see your friend?' asked Alice, curiously.

'Yes, we said goodbye... We promised to write.'

'Well, that's nice,' said Alice. She smoothed out a ribbon on one of Joanna's capes, sighing with satisfaction. 'I'm so glad we are returning!'

'You do seem glad. What were you discussing with Marie before I arrived?'

Anxious to hide her smiles, Alice focused tremendously on the ribbon. 'We spoke about the future and how each one of us has a different agenda for shaping our fortunes.'

CHAPTER THIRTEEN

Alice opened the shutters and morning's light poured into their apartment, brightening all their familiar objects. They'd arrived back in Poitiers so late the night before they'd gone to bed directly. Her eyes soaked up the clear blue sky and rejoiced at the sight of the trees dressed skimpily in frost. Last night's fires had been built so high the embers were still glowing in the grate.

Joanna stirred, shielding her eyes against the light. 'Ugh, draw the shutters over a bit,' she grumbled, 'until my eyes have adjusted. My goodness, it's warm in here! What a perfect day for hawking!'

'I've laid out your things,' said Alice, nodding towards her costume. 'I can help you into it, if you like, or perhaps you'd prefer the maid?'

'I'd rather you did it, please.'

The outfit was similar to the one she'd been wearing on that hateful day. Curiously, the attack hadn't put Joanna off hawking. If anything, she approached the sport with more determination.

Joanna made no objection to Alice accompanying her on the expedition. Alice herself was wearing a heavy woollen tunic and her hair was twisted in a turban. After Alice had buttoned her up, Joanna sat at the glass and angled a new feathered cap artfully on her head. *That cap would look ridiculous on me*, thought Alice, *yet it looks perfect on her*.

Joanna rested her gaze on Alice in the glass. 'Are you excited?'

'Oh, I shall enjoy being out-of-doors on such a day,' Alice replied, lightly. In fact, she'd have much preferred to spend the day in quiet contemplation. Perhaps take a gentle stroll in the woods later with Marie...

'My blood is pumping so fast around my body, I can scarcely catch my breath for excitement!' said Joanna. 'My senses are so alert I believe I am capable of anything. I feel most alive like this, as if I am an elemental thing, a part of nature and nothing — not even death — can harm me. I am composed of the very same matter as the horses, the hawks, their prey, even the forest foliage!'

In winter, Eleanor and her ladies went hawking without the customary knightly escort. The clear day induced a cheerful and relaxed atmosphere, and the ladies stood around chatting as the groomsmen brought out their horses. The falconer stood apart with his birds. Eleanor and Marie made their entrance last, both dressed in leather camouflage. Marie threw up her hands to Alice, as if to say, *what choice do we have?* She didn't care for the sport either. Alice's heart flushed with warmth.

In the absence of the noblemen, Eleanor let her vibrant hair hang loose, wearing only a pale green band and looking like a fairy queen. Her cheeks looked delicately flushed against her pale skin and her eyes were sparkling like crystals in the sunlight.

'Joanna, come ride alongside me!' she called.

Alice thought they resembled a pair of beautiful, bloodthirsty goddesses.

They trotted through the picnicking area, past the place where the tall trees had once sheltered Joanna's songbird. The horses broke into a canter then across a wide plain, stopping at the edge of a common land forest.

In wintertime, the court reserved exclusive hawking rights, so they could be assured of prey. Bush beaters from the encampment had gone before them to alarm the partridge and quail out of their hiding places. Flora went to work at once, flying high to observe her prey, before diving at breakneck speed, wings stuck together like a brush stroke. Having shed her initial queasiness about the slaughter, Joanna hunted with strategy and skill. Perhaps due to the clear day, fowl was so thick on the ground that the ladies had trouble keeping up with their hawks. Eleanor and Joanna worked as a team, with Eleanor commanding Flora and Joanna following closely to retrieve the spoils. It cost her not a thought to slit the throats of partridge now.

At midday they stopped for lunch, spreading fleeces on the forest floor and emptying out the contents of their carrier bags: treacle tarts, rough cheeses, roast beef, radishes, onions, chicken legs, grapes and a vat of purple wine. After eating, they went in pairs for a brisk walk. The queen did not allow them to go alone, or to venture out of sight, as the forests were notorious dwelling places for outlaws. They drank icy cold water from the stream. Joanna dug up a truffle with her freezing, bloodied hands.

'Ladies, let us return now to the castle!' Eleanor beckoned. 'We've caught more meat than we can eat, and it's getting…' A piercing screech halted her speech. Some ladies cried out in fright.

Alice's eyes searched wildly for the source of the noise. The sound was repeated — even louder than before — it didn't come from themselves. The thing was in close range but weirdly invisible. A pair of wings sliced across them. The colour and expanse were similar to Flora's.

'Flora?' Eleanor called, confused. But Flora shuffled on a branch just overhead. 'Ladies,' the queen cried, 'it's a wild falcon and may be aggressive! Call back your hawks!' She quickly pulled on her leather glove and called to Flora.

A hawk appeared out of nowhere. It dashed about in an angry frenzy, descending on their morning's carrion, attacking it with its beak and claws.

'Flora... No!' Eleanor commanded. But the huge maternal hawk swept across to cut off the wild intruder as it took off with a partridge squeezed in its talons. A ferocious battle ensued between the hawks, with the ladies powerless to do anything but gaze on in fascinated horror.

The wild hawk proved the stronger and Flora fell to the ground, wounded. She moaned and shivered like a human. One of her magnificent wings was rumpled and distorted.

'Fifi?' Joanna's voice rang out.

'Fifi!' Eleanor's echoed.

The ladies were uncomprehending.

'Didn't you recognize her?' Joanna cried in choked voice.

'Yes! That was Fifi,' Eleanor said.

'Shall I go after her?' asked Joanna.

'No, Joanna.' Eleanor stopped her. 'Let her go, she's wild now. She's gone savage.'

'But surely she can be retrained...?'

'No, you must let her go. She attacked her own mother.'

Joanna's face was wet with tears.

They returned in silence like a funeral procession. The falconer appeared out of nowhere at the forest's edge. 'What happened?'

Flora shuffled towards him, her yellow eyes pleading for comfort.

'She was attacked ... by another falcon,' said Eleanor. 'By Fifi.'

'That is most unusual,' the falconer observed. 'Then Fifi is alive?' His gaze appeared to search through the forest and penetrate to where the young falcon was feasting on the carrion. He returned his attention to Flora. He lifted her tenderly, his fingers probing her delicate bones. 'The wing will heal,' he said.

Joanna started sobbing and his eyes flicked across to her.

'You should be pleased, lady,' he said. 'The young falcon lives.'

'But she's gone bad,' sobbed Joanna. 'She attacked her own mother!'

'Not bad,' he said, matter-of-factly, 'just wild. She had to go wild to survive. She'll do as she pleases now.'

'Such a powerful omen must be carefully considered,' said Eleanor, as she dismounted. Her slender, gold-ringed fingers stroked Hero's silver coat, nervously. Her loose hair was like a bright crown around her pale face, and her eyes were glittering strangely.

Alice stared at her.

'Don't you see?' Eleanor said. 'It is an omen for the New Year.'

The falconer nodded sagely in agreement. 'The birds don't lie,' he agreed.

'The hawk is a symbol of nobility,' Eleanor said. 'The young one attacking its parent is highly irregular. It's a sign, ladies, that must be read. Take Hero back for me, please. I must go at once to pray for guidance.'

'Shall I accompany you, Mother?' asked Marie.

'No, my flower, I must go alone.'

That evening, Chretien de Troyes joined Marie and Alice in the Tower. Alice had almost forgotten Chretien's existence over the holiday and his name evoked only the slightest upset, like an unpleasant taste. She was sitting close to Marie when he arrived. Chretien stood with his back to the door, looking comically small in the grand arched doorway. He blinked at them shyly, his weak eyes straining to make them out.

Marie rushed forward to greet him, while Alice stretched out her feet before rising slowly. Alice averted her eyes when Marie embraced him. She wished she was not so free with her affections.

'Come, Chretien, sit with us! You see Alice is here!'

They exchanged a timid smile.

'We've had quite a day,' remarked Marie. 'Perhaps you heard about the hawking adventure this morning?'

He shook his head.

'You remember Joanna's falcon, Fifi, that went missing in the summer? Everyone had presumed she was dead. Well, just as we were packing up our picnic things, she appeared out of nowhere and attacked the carrion, and then she attacked Flora — her own mother! I'd never have recognized her as Fifi, but Joanna and Eleanor knew her, of course. It was most surprising and disturbing and … I can't say what else. My mother was beside herself and has been praying in the chapel ever since. She says such an event must be a profound omen. What do you think, Chretien?'

Chretien gave an impressed whistle. 'I've heard of this kind of omen. In the Prophesies of Merlin, there is a story where four birds are attached to the body of a large eagle. Three of them are attacking the parent with their talons while the fourth is pecking out its eyes. This prophesy is supposed to relate to one of the kings of ancient race and his royal offspring.'

'How marvellous!' exclaimed Marie. 'Imagine knowing such things! Chretien, your memory and intellect are simply astounding!'

Alice didn't understand the story or its relevance to their experience that morning, but she dared not speak in case they'd think her feeble-minded.

'It's not difficult to remember such a powerful image — or omen,' he said, modestly. 'The ancients always used the language of the birds to foresee the future. However, not many possess the skill nowadays to interpret it.'

'I suspect the falconer does,' said Marie. 'He seemed as alarmed as mother. Alice, what do you think?'

Alice was glad of the dusk hiding her discomfort. 'It was certainly frightening to observe,' she said. 'It seems so unnatural, a parent being attacked by its own child ... horrible.'

Chretien shook his head. 'These are strange times... Strange times indeed.'

CHAPTER FOURTEEN

The start of summer saw the return of many noblemen from their winter estates — among them Bertran de Born. One evening, as Joanna and Alice were sitting idly by a weak fire, Eleanor came to broach the subject with Joanna. 'I wondered if his presence would upset you?' she asked.

Joanna shrugged her petite shoulders. 'Bertran has done me no harm. Why should he not return to court?'

'Well, yes,' Eleanor agreed. 'It's just that people will talk, as I'm sure you know. People will gossip about what happened between you.'

Joanna blinked and her soft mouth set in a rigid line. Alice realized that Eleanor was worried that Joanna might tell people that it was, in fact, her son who had attacked Joanna and not Bertran — as everyone thought. Joanna must have realized it too, for she sighed and said, 'Let them gossip. I intend to stay silent on the matter, and I hope that will stop them. Besides, with Richard's being invested as count, I doubt that mine and Bertran's history will continue to fascinate.'

Eleanor looked relieved. She took Joanna's little hands and kissed her fingertips. 'I'll see to it that you and Bertran are kept apart,' she assured her. 'You shall have the very best place at Richard's banquet! You too, Alice.'

Joanna laughed with pleasure. Her laughter was sweet and infectious, and soon all three of them were smiling. 'So much has happened in the past year,' said Joanna. 'I feel quite old and weary with experience!'

'One grows up fast at court,' said Eleanor, wryly.

'Like Fifi,' said Joanna. 'She had to grow up fast in order to survive.'

Eleanor and her ladies had spent the past month making copious visits to the dressmaker to plan their summer wardrobes. They generally walked down together, testing the dressmaker's already limited patience extremely, with their clamour and bold demands. Summer fashions were usually both elaborate and flimsy, giving the ladies opportunity to show their figures to full advantage with the aim of attracting a wealthy husband. Apart from the usual May dances and courtship rituals, Eleanor had advised them each to have a special costume made up for the occasion of Richard's investiture as Count of Poitou at the end of May.

Richard was to receive the holy lance and standard of St Hilaire, and he was to be presented to the lords of Poitou as their future overlord. While Eleanor was busy making preparations with Richard, across the water, Henry was working industriously on the imminent coronation of young Henry with Princess Marguerite, due to take place in June. To apologize for his public outburst and humiliation of Richard at Christmas, Henry had agreed to let Richard be sworn in as count before his brother's coronation had taken place. Eleanor had managed to persuade him that it would be better if she and Richard stayed in Poitiers while the king organised Henry's coronation. This way, she tactfully avoided being implicated in the quarrel between Henry and Becket. It was still unclear to everyone how King Henry would manage the tradition of the Archbishop of Canterbury presiding over the coronation ceremony, when he and the archbishop weren't speaking.

Alice watched Joanna closely to see if she was still affected by the mention of young Henry's name, but she appeared unmoved. Many young lords and dashing-looking knights were arriving for Richard's investiture, and Joanna would surely have admirers among them. Alice hoped that she had put her past trauma behind her sufficiently to fall for someone eligible. She was sure that her niece — if she played her game correctly — should become engaged soon. With relief, she noted that Joanna responded to Jean's letters dutifully rather than eagerly. She kept much closer contact with the young nun she'd met at Fontevrault — a relationship of which Alice heartily approved.

So far, Alice was happy with the progress they were making at court and was grateful for the new-found respectability they had found as Eleanor's attending-ladies. She was confident that Joanna's misadventure with the prince would melt away from the collective memory, like winter snow from the mountaintops.

When Joanna went to the dressmaker now, she gave her orders with confidence. 'A low-cut bosom, but tight-fitting on the buttocks,' she'd command.

Alice ordered yet another black gown, with only a fuller, stiffer skirt to mark the occasion of Richard's investiture. Joanna went out riding so often that her skin was sun-kissed a delicate gold and her auburn hair was streaked with lighter tones. Alice's complexion was pale and unhealthy-looking from spending too much time indoors. She noticed small, welcome changes in Joanna. She was more composed and secretive, less likely to express her feelings readily. She carried herself with the poise of one aware of her own beauty. As well as excelling at singing, dancing and hawking, Joanna was finally mastering her letters — thanks to Marie's patience and perseverance. Alice realized that Joanna would make a cultivated and appealing wife for any nobleman.

The ladies rose at cock's crow on the day of Richard's

investiture and gathered in the chamber offering most light. After attending to Eleanor's magnificent robes, their maids came rushing forth with a variety of colourful dresses, veils and ribbons.

Joanna succumbed to Alice's scrutiny on this special occasion.

'Just let me comb your hair again to bring it into shine,' Alice said.

'Well, don't disturb the curls,' Joanna grumbled.

Her dress had a grass-green bodice with a striking, scarlet skirt. Lots of the other ladies had opted for the pastel shades of early summer, so Joanna stood out among them like a rare bird.

Clever girl, thought Alice, tying her mother's amethysts around her throat.

'Oh, not those!' Joanna protested.

'But these are perfect with the dress…'

'I shall wear no jewels today,' said Joanna, decidedly.

'Really, Joanna, you are most whimsical,' grumbled Alice. She shrugged. 'Very well, your neck is pretty enough.'

Joanna smiled gratefully.

Little puffs of cloud were floating in a perfect blue sky as the ladies and townspeople made their way down the horse-chestnut and elm-lined street towards the abbey of St Hilaire. Some of them carried tiny paper umbrellas to keep the sun from their faces as they followed Eleanor's carriage on foot.

'How silly they look,' scoffed Joanna.

'You would do well to keep your face out of the sun,' warned Alice. 'You'll be sorry when you're older and your skin is all wrinkled like mine…'

Eleanor, Richard and Marie alighted from their carriage and stood before the abbey gates. Eleanor and Richard were wearing splendid ivory and gold embroidered robes and delicate gold crowns. Marie's ivory costume was simple, but she wore the elaborately jewelled tiara of a princess. Alice thought she looked like an ancient Greek goddess with the tiny jewels in her glossy black hair.

Eleanor drew her ladies around her, and Alice was glad of the vantage point. Behind them, the lay people strained to get the best view. The path leading to the abbey was lined on either side with the nobly attired and distinguished-looking barons of Poitiers, their flying banners overhead. Each nobleman held a shield on which was painted a different animal or bird.

All fell silent when the bell rang twelve times. The abbey doors creaked open and an army of knights spilled out. After them came the Bishop of Poitiers and Archbishop of Bordeaux — resplendent in costly vestments. Eleanor and Richard then proceeded through the barons. On reaching the bishop and archbishop, Richard bent on one knee to receive from them the holy Lance and Standard of St Hilaire. The rite of passage was followed by a solemn mass in the abbey accompanied by sacred choral music, designed to draw tears from the greatest of sinners. Marie was standing up front with the knights, tears streaming down her cheeks. Joanna was likewise moved and Alice — always prepared — offered her a linen cloth. She wished she could offer similar comfort to Marie.

Viewed from behind, the thirteen-year-old newly minted Count looked broad-shouldered and manly. Only when he turned, his smooth, hairless chin and unfurrowed brow betrayed his true age. Alice considered the serious role he was about to undertake. These same barons who were bowing their heads in prayer and thanksgiving were renowned for their rebelliousness, even their ruthlessness towards their overlords.

Alice saw in their faces the same calculating, closed expression she read on the faces of the most shrewdly political courtiers. Richard may have been divinely chosen as future Duke, but if his policies did not bend to their agendas they would cause trouble. His investiture as Count of Poitiers was only the beginning of a long and fractious relationship, as complicated as a game of chess. As Richard was only thirteen, it would be another two years before they would pay homage to him as Duke of Aquitaine. Much could happen in two years.

After mass, Richard invited everyone to return to the castle for celebrations of jousting and feasting. The ladies dried their eyes and carefully smoothed their hair. Alice brushed some specks of mud from Joanna's skirt. 'Look at me?' Using her cloth, she cleaned the charcoal bleeding around her eyes. Joanna drew away from her, linking arms with Lady Rosemary — who looked every bit the English rose in her peach, silk dress.

'Are you coming to the banquet?' Rosemary asked.

'Yes, of course! Let's sit together,' said Joanna, clearly eager to escape Alice.

'I did not think you would attend,' said Rosemary. 'I suppose you know that Bertran de Born is to perform?'

'What Bertran de Born does is no concern of mine,' Joanna said, breezily.

'I'm so glad to hear it!' said Rosemary. 'You must sit with me and advise me. Bertran is pestering me, you know. It's really irritating, especially with all these knights and lords about. What if they get the wrong impression and think we are together? Imagine if they confused me with one of his past conquests? Promise you'll sit with me, Joanna, and ward him off. He liked you once, before ... well. Perhaps you could divert him for me?'

Alice followed and sat next to them at Eleanor's table. She found herself directly across from a knight called Hugh de Montel She noticed how his eyes kept flicking across to Joanna. Alice quickly introduced herself as Joanna's aunt — her guardian — to catch his attention. It was hard to ascertain his age, though he was certainly older than Joanna by at least a decade. His eyes were a light, sugary brown and his nose arched at the nostrils, a sign of noble birth. He answered her questions about his position and prospects politely, while she subtly informed him of the rich estate herself and Joanna came from. Although he looked often at Joanna, she never returned his gaze. Alice applauded her niece for her composure, knowing that she must be straining to listen in on their conversation. Alice gleaned as much information as she could without appearing too nosy or grasping. She found him to be both a good listener and a gentleman.

The boards were cleared aside for dancing and neither Rosemary nor Joanna sat down again all evening. Alice, on the other hand, did not stand up. Even with a heavily outnumbered ratio of male to female dancers, she was not asked to dance.

'You prefer not to dance, Lady Alice?' Chretien de Troyes said kindly, coming especially to address her.

'My dancing days are over,' she replied.

'Mine too.' He sat beside her. They watched the dancers silently. Marie was also in demand as a partner. Neither said another word till Alice bid him goodnight.

Joanna followed her out and they undressed together by candlelight.

'So, what's he like?' Joanna asked, unable to conceal her interest.

'Aha!' said Alice, teasing. 'I wondered why you'd come to bed so early.'

'Well?'

'His table-manners are impeccable,' Alice replied.

Joanna laughed giddily. 'Yes, but what's he like? You were speaking with him all through dinner. I only had one dance with him and we were interrupted. We barely spoke.'

Alice considered. 'I wouldn't call him a charming sort of fellow — like Bertran de Born. He seems ... serious.'

'Ugh! Why does everyone keep speaking to me of Bertran de Born?' said Joanna, impatiently. 'I care nothing for him! What impression did you get of Hugh de Montel's character?'

'I got a very good impression of his prospects. He's to inherit an estate on large grounds with lakes and forests. He spoke of many servants and fine chambers.' Joanna stared at her, and Alice knew she'd made a great error. She'd come across as greedy. She hurriedly tried to retract. 'He must be a passionate sort of fellow, for he stared at you all night.' She fumbled with the ribbons on Joanna's bodice.

'Leave it,' Joanna said, sharply. 'I'll do it myself.'

Alice withdrew, cursing herself for her careless speech. She wanted Joanna's future secured — and soon — for many reasons. Not least because the girl would then be out of harm's way. She also knew that Joanna was not the kind of girl to be content living without the luxury of fine things. Of course, she hoped, for herself, that she would accompany Joanna to her new estate, but that was not foremost in her thoughts. She simply wanted security for them both — was that too much to ask?

CHAPTER FIFTEEN

Eleanor ordered her ladies to prepare for a trip to Fontevrault. The weather being clement and the days long, they could leave at their leisure after breakfast and arrive at the abbey before nightfall. Some of them grumbled furiously behind her back.

'I cannot believe she's taking us to the nunnery when there's so much to entertain here at court!'

Alice and Joanna were both delighted by the prospect; Joanna couldn't wait to be reunited with her friend, and Alice embraced the idea of leaving behind the vanities of the court for the soulfulness of Fontevrault. Also, she would have Marie to herself, without Chretien.

'My husband is sending one of his stewards from England with a donation for the abbey in thanksgiving for Richard's investiture and Henry's upcoming coronation. I must be there when he arrives to put my seal to the gift,' Eleanor explained. 'I apologise for removing you from court at this joyous time, ladies, but we mustn't forget to give praise and thanks to our Lord.'

Alice and Joanna changed into dark clothing and helped to fasten each other's veils.

By midday, the party was well on its way to Fontevrault.

They arrived in time for the evensong sung by the nuns, followed by a simple supper of bread, cheese and milk. They slipped back easily into the routine of silent meals punctuated by prayer and long days of quiet meditation. Joanna found plenty to entertain around the grounds this time and spent all her time outdoors with Heloise.

Alice and Marie took long walks together and Alice felt physically lighter, as if a burden of responsibility had been lifted from her shoulders.

On one of these walks, Marie spoke to Alice of her husband and the two children she had left behind. She had forsaken every possible luxury and comfort to pursue her poetic endeavours. She spoke with sadness of her children — but she knew that they were in more capable hands. 'I was no use as a wife or as a mother,' she explained, 'for I always yearned to work. Someday I shall return to them, when my work is done.'

'Did your husband mind your leaving?'

'Of course, he did,' Marie said. 'But what choice did he have when Eleanor summoned me to attend her at court? I doubt he'll ever forgive me. Or her.'

'Are you sorry you left?' Alice ventured.

'No,' Marie said. 'It was my decision. Mother would never have forced me if I wished to remain at home.'

'Was it not enough to live in luxury and security?' Alice wondered.

'It was not enough to satisfy me,' Marie said. 'My work was more important than anything else.'

Now Alice understood better why Marie spent all that time with Chretien. She looped her arm through Marie's and felt a fluttering of gratitude in her heart. Her husband's loss was Alice's gain; it would be a sin to keep so vibrant a person as Marie hidden away.

They bent their heads together to step through the low, carved entrance of the orchard. Young apples and pears hung like jewels from the ancient fruit trees.

'I do believe this is the most peaceful place on earth!' exclaimed Alice, blissfully.

The long shadow of a man emerged out of the trees onto their path and halted before them. 'Caught!' He laughed, pleasantly. He held out a cap full of lush cherries.

'My word, they look delicious!' said Marie.

'I was starving after supper,' he said, smiling.

They recognised him as King Henry's steward, Manasse.

'I expect you are offered more meat at Henry's table,' smiled Marie.

'You find more of everything at Henry's table!' Manasse agreed.

Alice did not welcome the intrusion and held herself stiffly apart, remaining in hostile silence.

'Would you like to walk with us?' Marie offered. Manasse accepted gratefully. 'Excellent! You must show us where you robbed those from.'

'Follow me,' Manasse said. He ducked down through the trees.

'How are things at Henry's court?' Marie asked, pointedly.

'Things are bad. I suppose you've heard of this quarrel with Thomas Becket?'

'Yes, we kept Christmas with Henry at Chinon,' said Marie, rolling her eyes.

'Ah, well, then you know.' Manasse gestured as if to say he'd not have disclosed anything they hadn't already known.

'Go on,' invited Marie. Manasse glanced at Alice. Marie nodded. 'Total discretion there,' she assured.

They arrived at a magnificent cherry tree with branches outstretched, generously laden with fruit.

'What a glorious tree!' said Alice, breaking her silence.

Manasse continued speaking as they helped themselves. 'The young king's coronation is due to take place on the fourteenth of June, but the king remains at odds with the archbishop.

Henry has petitioned the Archbishop of York to preside over the coronation instead.'

Marie broke into a fit of coughing. Alice rubbed her back until it stopped.

'Shall I find some water?' Manasse asked.

'I'm fine, just a cherry gone down wrong! Do go on.'

'Everyone is angry, most of all the Pope — he is furious with Henry! What's worse, it's rumoured that Princess Marguerite will not be crowned alongside young Henry.'

'I beg your pardon? Surely that's not true?' Marie was amazed. 'It would enrage my father if Marguerite was not crowned.'

'As I said, it is only a rumour. However, rumours about Henry tend to be true. The rift between the king and archbishop is growing worse. Henry is in foul humour, but he stubbornly insists on going ahead with the coronation despite all obstacles.'

They resumed walking, Marie with the steward and Alice behind.

Soft shafts of golden sunlight falling through the trees caressed their faces, and a full moon came bouncing early into the blue sky. King Henry's court seemed worlds away in this dreamy setting, and it was difficult to imagine such distant tales of woe. Only Manasse's honest countenance gave substance to the tale.

'Surely Henry and Becket will come to an agreement soon,' said Marie. 'It benefits neither one to have the quarrel continue. Henry's plans are hampered, and Becket lives in exile. It cannot go on like this. Have you told my mother what you have told us?'

'The queen was informed of everything on her arrival two days ago,' Manasse said.

That explained why Eleanor had locked herself away in the chapel.

'She has much to pray for now,' muttered Marie. 'I cannot imagine what my father would do if princess Marguerite were not crowned...' They entered the courtyard through one of the cloisters. 'Would young Henry not refuse to be crowned without the princess?'

'He doesn't seem to care, so long as he is crowned at the allotted time. The prince is vain and spoilt.'

'Yes, we know something of his character. He stayed with us last summer. Alice's beautiful niece fell prey to his charms, and it nearly cost her her reputation.'

'She's not the only young lady he has undone nor, I fear, will she be the last. The king indulged him recklessly as a youth, and now he is most conceited.' Manasse turned to Alice. 'I hope your niece has found a husband since?'

Alice cleared her throat. 'Not yet, but I hope she'll soon be betrothed.'

'Good, you must take her out of harm's way,' he said.

'I shall not rest easy until she's safely married,' said Alice. 'It's a constant source of worry, sir, and I am growing weary. Joanna — my niece — is a most extraordinary girl and deserves every happiness.'

CHAPTER SIXTEEN

Scandalous reports reached Poitiers about the young Henry's coronation. Contrary to tradition, his father had gone ahead with the ceremony without the Archbishop of Canterbury. He had also enraged King Louis of France by having his son crowned without Princess Marguerite. Both Louis and the Pope were furious — the Pope threatened to excommunicate Henry if he did not make amends with Becket. To add to the insult, the young king was rumoured to have made his father wait on him at the coronation banquet — making Henry seem a fool.

Eleanor avoided being implicated in the botched coronation by remaining at Poitiers with Richard. She secretly dispatched a message to Henry asking him to explain his position on princess Marguerite and urging him to make up with Becket on pain of excommunication and eternal damnation. The reply arrived just as Eleanor was sitting down to banquet. She hurried from the hall back to the Tower and with trembling hands, read the message aloud to her ladies.

Henry addressed the question of Marguerite — saying he intended to have another coronation for the young king and his queen with Becket presiding. He said he intended to make amends with Becket and had invited the archbishop to return to England and spend a few days as his guest at court before taking up his position as archbishop.

'Praise be to God!' said Eleanor, relieved and visibly moved. 'We must celebrate! Call all our troubadours and musicians. Ladies, let us dance and make merry!'

Alice gave Joanna total freedom now, and she noticed Hugh de Montel attending to her during the night's festivities.

The next morning, Joanna burst into their shared chamber just as Alice was rising.

'Goodness, what's happened?' Alice said, alarmed.

Joanna flung herself on the bed. 'I hardly know! Oh, do I look all right?' Her hands flew to her face, her hair. 'Hugh de Montel met me on my walk this morning! He came to meet me on purpose.' She jumped up to check herself in the glass. 'Oh, I should have listened to you, Alice, I should at least have worn a cap. Look at my hair! I must take more care of my appearance when I go out. He said he always watched me from his window!'

'Really?' Alice wrapped a shawl around her night shift and came to stand beside Joanna. 'You walked with him alone?'

'Yes, but in full view of the castle guards. Don't worry, Alice, it was thoroughly respectable. I behaved most properly. I didn't even speak until after he had spoken…'

'Very good. Now that he has walked with you once, I believe he'll wish to do so again. He was probably building up courage as he watched you from the window. I believe Hugh de Montel intends to court you, Joanna!'

Their eyes met in mutual excitement.

'I intend to be most ladylike! But, Alice, I am afraid…'

'Your natural modesty causes you to fear matrimony? Don't let fear stop you, Joanna, have courage.'

The next morning, Joanna dressed with care in a light brown dress and matching velvet cap. Just as Alice predicted, Hugh was waiting for her in the exact same place. When Joanna returned, she was clutching a violet which Hugh had given to her.

'How old do you think he is?' she asked Alice. 'What are his likes and dislikes? Do you think he reads or writes?'

'I doubt it,' said Alice. 'He was trained as a knight and not educated as a scholar.'

'Do you think he killed many infidels?' asked Joanna.

'I could not say.'

The other ladies commented jealously on Hugh's favour for Joanna, and Alice could see that Joanna was enjoying the attention. Joanna took to hawking at every opportunity, seeking release. She became a ferocious hawker. Alice would have been concerned had Joanna not behaved so properly otherwise. Joanna had become the perfect lady, elegant and extraordinarily beautiful, with impeccable manners and speech. Her dress sense was fresh, but captivating, to match her personality.

Hugh de Montel was clearly smitten.

The days were so hot that all outdoor activity was carried out before noon, when the ladies returned indoors. Alice, Joanna and Eleanor's other maids would sponge the queen with cool rosewater and draw the shutters so she could enjoy a restful nap before the evening's entertainment. Alice was engaged in needlework when she saw Rosemary jump up and look out of the window.

'Joanna, come quick and look!' Rosemary cried.

'What is it?'

'Look there!' Rosemary pointed to a brightly dressed group entering the gates. 'How gay they look! I wonder where they're from.'

Alice saw Joanna turn pale and followed her gaze. It was Jean.

'My goodness, Joanna, are you all right?' Rosemary asked. 'You've turned quite pale.'

Joanna's forehead was shiny with perspiration. She blinked and quickly came to her senses. 'Blasted sun is so hot, that's all. Let's close the shutters.'

'I wonder where they've come from,' said Rosemary, excited.

'I believe they're musicians from Chinon,' Joanna said, casually enough. 'I think I recognise some of them.'

'Marvellous!' Rosemary clapped her hands. 'We'll have dancing tonight!'

'Not I. I'm afraid I must go and lie down,' said Joanna. 'The heat is causing me to feel most faint. Please tell Eleanor I am unwell and won't be attending banquet.'

Alice followed her to their chamber.

'Close the door please, Alice.'

'Of course. Are you ill?'

'Just overheated, nothing to worry about,' Joanna answered, vaguely.

'I told you to cover your head when you go riding,' Alice scolded. 'I notice your friends — the musicians from Chinon — have arrived. The boy, Jean, will be looking for you. What shall I tell him?'

'Tell him I am indisposed at present and unable to see him.'

'Unable or unwilling?' said Alice, most gently.

'Perhaps both?' Joanna replied, truthfully.

'Very well, I shall let him know.'

'I'm afraid Eleanor was too perturbed to notice your absence,' sighed Alice when she returned to the chamber. 'They brought evil tidings from the English court.'

Joanna sat up. 'What do you mean?'

'You remember how happy Eleanor was that Henry had agreed to make amends with Thomas Becket? Well, shortly after the young king's coronation, Becket was summoned to England to negotiate the constitutions of Clarendon. After Becket's ship docked at Sandwich, they travelled on to Clarendon by horseback. They decided to stop en route at the young king's new castle at Winchester — for Becket was eager to see his old pupil again. However, at the young king's castle, a tragedy occurred. Instead of welcoming his old tutor with kisses, Becket's entourage was greeted with a shower of arrows — one of which proved fatal to Becket's oldest advisor...'

'Oh, no, that's awful!'

'Yes. Dreadful,' Alice agreed. 'Being highly suspicious and distrustful by nature, the archbishop concluded that the old King Henry was colluding with the son against him and had invited him back under false pretences to take his life. He fled with his men back to Sandwich and set sail again for France and safer ground. To make matters worse, Henry won't force the young king to apologise — although Becket demands it — which consolidates Becket's belief that father and son were plotting against him. It really is the most appalling mess.'

'Why should young Henry have attacked Becket?' Joanna asked, puzzled.

'It's likely that the young king was unaware of Becket's arrival and his men acted on their own and irresponsibly. The young king's court is a haphazard place, presided over by reckless, overly-indulged youths, like the prince himself.'

'Poor Eleanor,' said Joanna, 'she was so pleased when the matter between Henry and Becket seemed to be resolved.'

'Henry has dispatched envoys begging Becket to return to reconcile their differences, insisting that the incident was an unfortunate misunderstanding. So far, the messages have fallen on deaf ears.'

Alice undressed quickly and got into bed. She lay awake long into the night, listening to the strange silence; it was as though a death had occurred, the castle was so still and serious.

CHAPTER SEVENTEEN

All the court waited outside in the blistering afternoon heat, eagerly anticipating Eleanor's return from Paris. She'd left Richard in charge, a gesture to honour his new title as Count of Poitiers, while visiting King Louis with Marie in the hopes of reconciling the two kings and Becket by arranging a second coronation with the archbishop presiding.

Richard had organised Eleanor's homecoming. She had sent a cautious message, informing them that — although the news was good — she wished to avoid appearing vitriolic. This was God's victory — after all — not theirs, so nothing too lavish was prepared. The troubadours and musicians had arranged subtle compositions. In the kitchens, the cooks were busy stuffing pheasants with herb butter — hearty, wholesome fare — nothing fancy. But they'd added precious ginger to the ale and had rolled in a vat of Eleanor's favourite wine from a monastery in Burgundy. She would enjoy these simple pleasures after a tiring journey. Everyone wore simple clothing, but with pretty rose-garlands in their hair which had started to wilt in the sun. They were relieved when the scout galloped down with his flag to indicate the carriage had been sighted.

Eleanor and Marie looked dusty and weary. Alice could see the strain in Marie's face and knew it must have been particularly difficult for her to negotiate between her natural father and her stepfather. She'd need to indulge in music and laughter to recover.

Eleanor mustered enough strength to make a speech. 'It is my pleasure to inform the court that Henry of England has met with the Archbishop of Canterbury, Thomas Becket, and an agreement has been reached.'

The courtiers cheered and clapped.

'King Henry crossed the channel and met the archbishop on the 22nd of July at Fréteval. It was witnessed by King Louis, our daughter, Marie and the Archbishop of Rouen, as well as myself — Queen Eleanor of Aquitaine. Henry threw his arms around Becket and begged him to reconcile and forget their differences. The archbishop agreed to return to England and preside over the real coronation of the young king Henry and Princess Marguerite.'

She stepped down to great cheering.

Alice watched as Hugh de Montel stepped towards Joanna. 'Lady Joanna?'

'Hugh!' Joanna kissed his cheeks, making him blush. 'Isn't it wonderful!' Her lovely eyes were bright with tears.

'It's a wonderful outcome!' he agreed. 'Wonderful too that your hawking partner is returned to you in such good spirits! Would you care to walk with me?' He offered his arm.

As a formality, Joanna looked to Alice, who nodded. Couples who were officially courting would often take a turn around the front lawn or else the adjoining courtyard. This courtship was being conducted formally and properly ... safely — in full view of everyone — and Alice found comfort in that.

Just as Joanna and Hugh were turning into the courtyard, a beautiful steed rode in with an impressive rider, his flowing black hair matching his horse's shiny coat; his scarlet waistcoat fluttering in the breeze. Alice saw Joanna's hand clench Hugh's arm. The rider was Bertran de Born. He dismounted and handed his groom a franc to lead the horse away. He gave Joanna the faintest nod and smirked as he walked past.

A few weeks later, Eleanor summoned her ladies to sit with her beneath the blood-red roses she'd brought back from the Holy Land while on crusade with her first husband, King Louis. Blooms the colour of pomegranate had spread from a small tree along an entire wall, filling the air with sweet, exotic perfume. Eleanor had changed into a dress so pale that her narrow form was outlined against the light. Her magnificent auburn hair was hanging loose. Alice and the rest of the ladies had shed both their headdresses and their footwear in the heat. Marie's dress of pale blue silk contrasted prettily with the vibrant, red background. Joanna had climbed up the stone ledge and stood precariously balanced as she tied ribbons onto thorny branches.

Eleanor lit a fat beeswax candle under the statue of the Virgin — queen of the roses — planted at the foot of the tree. The ladies drew silently close around her and Joanna lowered herself gracefully from the ledge to join her in prayer.

Their prayers were offered up for Henry, who had fallen gravely ill with a tertian fever during the trip to meet with Becket. So ill, it was feared he would die. Eleanor was terrified his soul would pass from the world before he'd had a chance to reinstate Becket. In all the years they'd been married, she'd grown to depend on Henry's robust constitution. It was the first time she'd known him to be ill, and she suspected Henry's illness was some kind of punishment for the way he'd treated God's shepherd. The planned reinstalment of Becket as archbishop would have to be delayed, as Henry was simply too ill to oversee it.

After offering their prayers, the ladies relaxed and chatted as bunches of burgundy grapes were passed around. Lady Rosemary was questioned about Bertran, Joanna about Hugh. Both ladies said they were confident of a proposal. They all agreed that Joanna couldn't find a finer fellow than Hugh. Over the course of the summer, he'd proven himself to be as chivalrous a courtier as he was a brave knight. Apart from that, he was both rich and handsome. The ladies agreed that he brought out Joanna's softer side and thought they were perfectly matched. Joanna blushed with pleasure as they complimented Hugh.

'Imagine the pretty babes you'd have together!' said Marie. 'What a fine, privileged life you'll lead. Best of all you'd have a companion you could speak with on the same level, for certainly he is easy-going and would not restrict you. Clearly he adores you!'

Joanna beamed with pleasure. 'Except ... but it is nothing.'

'No, no, you must tell us!' Marie said. 'Except what?'

'It's such a small thing, it hardly matters,' said Joanna. 'But, at the start of summer — when we first started courting — Hugh said he loved nothing more than to see me perform. However, recently I noticed that he seemed withdrawn and silent after watching me. When I broached the subject with him, at first, he denied it, but then he admitted that it disturbed him to think of other men watching me.'

'A-ha! So, he's jealous!' said Rosemary.

'Possibly,' said Joanna. 'I reminded him that I belong to no man and am no man's possession. He agreed and asked me to forgive him. But then, later, when we were speaking of something else entirely, he said that when he married, he hoped his wife would be content to stay at home with him and their children and not be desirous of other society and entertainment. I could not help but think he was alluding to our earlier conversation.'

'Of course he was!' said Marie. 'Did you expect your husband would let you continue to entertain at court after you were married? He'll spirit you away and hide you from the world. You cannot have it all, I'm afraid.'

'Then it's as I suspected,' sighed Joanna. 'I shall have to choose between the two.'

'On the bright side, remember you are not alone,' advised Marie. 'All women make sacrifices when they become wives; it's a fact that cannot be altered.'

Their conversation was interrupted by a messenger whose puffy face was shiny with perspiration after riding in the hot sun. King Henry was out of danger.

Eleanor's eyes filled instantly. 'My lord is recovered,' she said, thrilled. 'I must go to him. We must give thanks to God! Ladies, gather your things!'

Alice was busy packing when Joanna burst into their room. 'Oh, Alice! You'll never guess what has happened. Hugh de Montel has proposed, and I've said yes!'

'My goodness, oh, my goodness.' Alice flapped about, alarmed. 'How happy you must be!'

'I don't know what I'm feeling,' said Joanna. 'It all happened so quickly!'

'My goodness,' said Alice, again. 'He really did propose? Then it's really happening. It's what you want, Joanna, isn't it?'

'Yes, I believe so. What do you think, Alice? Do you think I should have accepted him so quickly? Does it seem rash, or ... unseemly?' She screwed up her nose at the word.

Alice smiled. 'I'm happy if you are happy, Joanna,' she said. 'I won't be the one marrying him. He seems a most worthy man, but then you know him much better than I.'

'He does seem worthy, doesn't he? And yet, Alice, I've known him only these past three months. Is it sufficient time, I wonder, to pick a husband?'

'He is not a piece of fruit you're plucking. At least you've had the opportunity to observe him at close quarters these past few months. Many brides don't have that advantage.'

'It's true the time we've spent has been intense.' Joanna brightened then frowned again with doubt. 'Hugh doesn't know everything about me. I have concealed my bad qualities from him, only shown him my good side. What if he finds something out about my person and my past he doesn't like and he decides not to have me after all? Do you think I should tell him about what happened last summer? He's bound to hear about it sooner or later.'

Alice turned away. 'I hardly think that would be wise, Joanna, do you? Besides, what is there to tell? You did nothing wrong…'

'Yes, it would hardly be wise,' Joanna repeated, slowly. She rubbed her temples with eyes squeezed shut as if to relieve tension — or solve some great problem.

'Don't worry about that now,' said Alice, briskly. 'Just rejoice in the moment! It's really the most marvellous news. Fancy getting a marriage proposal from so impressive a knight. You should be most happy!'

'Yes, it is marvellous. I should be happy, shouldn't I? I am happy!' Joanna's face lit up again. 'We agreed to announce our engagement at tonight's banquet. Rosemary will be so jealous!'

'Oh goodness, how late is the day? asked Alice. 'We'd better call the maid to get you ready. You must look your finest for your engagement banquet.'

Joanna lingered.

'Well, I'm not going to call her, looking like this!' said Alice. 'Run along, Joanna, and call her now.'

'I was wondering, Alice, if you'd do me a favour.'

'Of course — anything — what is it?'

Joanna cast her eyes over Alice. 'Would you mind dressing up too a little? Just for this special occasion. Would you let me choose something of Mama's for you to wear?'

Alice felt instant anxiety.

'Please, Alice. You are my one relation and my guardian, and you too will be introduced to and congratulated by everyone. I only ask that you wear something to celebrate the occasion and make me proud.'

'Fine,' Alice said, resigned. 'I see no harm in it. If it makes you happy, Joanna, dress me up as you wish!'

'Truly?'

'Why not?'

'Thank you, Alice!'

Joanna embraced her. Alice felt sadness rising through her joy.

'Now, please do as I say and call the maid before it's too late,' Alice said, turning away to hide her tears.

Joanna called back from the doorway, 'I should have got engaged a long time ago if I'd known it would persuade you to dress up!'

'For one night only, Joanna!'

'Very well, it's better than nothing.'

The maid fussed over Joanna for an age. She made her hair up into an elaborate style, piled high on her head, pinned with tiny, sparkling jewels. The style suited her apple-shaped face and showed off her dainty ears and beautiful features.

Even as the maid worked, though, Joanna was pulling out her mama's old dresses and jewellery for Alice to try on. She made Alice try at least a half dozen before she was happy. It was one of Carole's maternity gowns. They both agreed it gave the occasion even greater meaning.

'We are all three of us linked tonight,' said Joanna. 'Mama will be present too now, in a way.'

'Yes, Joanna dear, I remember her well in this dress,' Alice agreed. 'I can feel my sister close. She would be so proud of you.' Alice swallowed back her tears.

The dress was a simple, voluminous grey silk, with pretty embroidery on the bodice and sleeves making it suitable for evening wear.

'You do have an enviable figure for your age,' said Joanna, for the folds of silk hung well off Alice's thin frame. Joanna tied a jade brooch at the neck, of which Alice approved. The overall effect was elegant and understated.

Joanna's dress was an emerald shade — drawing out the gold flecks in her eyes. The maid had managed to tame Alice's hair into a neat top-bun over which a veil was draped. She'd even allowed Joanna to dust her hot cheeks with chalk and tint her lips with cherry paste.

Eleanor was delighted by the news of the engagement.

'Richard holds Hugh de Montel in the highest regard,' she said. 'I did not wish to influence your decision by speaking too highly of him, but I think you've made an excellent choice.'

Joanna, Hugh and Alice were given pride-of-place next to Eleanor, Richard and Marie at banquet.

'You look nice,' Marie said, noticing Alice's new dress. 'I've never seen you in this colour, it suits you well!'

Alice, though she shrugged off the compliment, was pleased. 'Hardly nice,' she laughed, 'but respectable at least... We said we would make a special effort on this most special of occasions.'

'Well, then, you look effortlessly elegant,' Marie insisted.

'Thank you,' Alice accepted. 'It is a look, however, that takes hours of effort to achieve!'

'Quite.'

They both laughed.

Eleanor began by informing the court of Henry's recovery and asking that they bow their heads in silent prayer and thanksgiving. After, she asked Joanna and Hugh to stand as she announced their engagement.

'It brings me the greatest pleasure to announce the engagement of our beautiful daughter, Lady Joanna of Agen to Sir Hugh de Montel. We congratulate them heartily and join together in wishing them every blessing and happiness for their future. May good fortune guide their way!'

All the court saluted them. Only Bertran de Born — his face clouded with ill humour — slipped from the hall.

At first opportunity, Rosemary left her seat and snuck up behind to pinch Joanna on the arm. 'So, you're to be married before me,' she pouted. 'I'll forgive you on one condition.'

'What's that?'

'That you make me your maiden attendant and I get to choose my own costume!'

'Agreed!'

'Have you set a date?' Rosemary asked.

'We are only just engaged,' Joanna laughed. 'Give us time!'

'It won't be long,' Hugh volunteered. 'I'm to return to run my late father's estate this winter, and I hope to take my lovely bride with me.'

'We'll miss you, Lady Joanna,' one of the other ladies said, sincerely. 'Sir, you take one of the greatest jewels of this court away with you.'

'A great jewel and the light of my life,' Hugh agreed.

'Your work is complete,' Marie whispered to Alice. 'You'll have to cease worrying over Joanna once and for all! She has made an excellent match.'

'Yes, I suppose I shall,' sighed Alice. 'Not until after the wedding, though; there will be much to prepare for that.'

'You're incorrigible!' laughed Marie. 'The only problem you'll have then is how to occupy yourself.'

CHAPTER EIGHTEEN

Eleanor left court to join her husband on a pilgrimage to the shrine of Rocamadour in Quercy and on their return, Henry stopped briefly at Poitiers to conduct business in the Duchy. It was clear to everyone at court that he still saw himself as Aquitaine's overlord and there were rumours that he had wielded his power ruthlessly over the barons, causing great resentment.

His rash undertakings also clearly infuriated Eleanor and Richard. Luckily, his sojourn lasted only a few days, as he had to go and meet Becket at Chaumont to reaffirm their agreement. Becket was to be issued a safe conduct to return to Canterbury and resume his episcopal duties.

Tired after her travels, Eleanor was to remain at Poitiers while Richard accompanied his father to Chaumont. Eleanor's narrow frame looked frail after four weeks of fasting on gridle bread and water. Her ladies bestowed every possible comfort to restore her to better health and spirits, and by the time Richard returned she was much better.

Alice gathered with the others to hear what had passed between Henry and Becket. Becket had agreed to return to Canterbury the following month.

'Was the archbishop more amiable this time?' Alice asked.

'They were both amicable enough,' said Richard, slowly. 'Theirs is a strange, volatile relationship, however, liable to take any unexpected turn.'

'That's most true,' sighed Eleanor. 'They're both as stubborn as mules.'

'For example,' Richard said, 'when Thomas Becket was about to depart, he laid a hand on Father's shoulder and said, "My lord, my mind tells me that I will never again see you in this life."'

'What an odd thing to say!' Eleanor said, dismayed.

'Well, Father certainly thought so, for he asked Becket directly if he thought Father a traitor. Becket's reply was, "God forbid, my lord."'

'How odd,' said Eleanor. 'Why would Becket say such a thing? He must be even more paranoid than we thought. Well, in time he'll realise he was mistaken.'

'Yes, Mama,' agreed Richard. 'Hopefully this whole unfortunate episode is at an end.'

The castle was quieter now, as many of the noblemen had returned to their estates for winter. Hugh de Montel had delayed his departure as long as possible, but he could not put it off forever. The evening before he left, he had asked Joanna to walk out with him one last time.

When Joanna returned, Alice noticed that she seemed out of sorts. 'What is the matter, my dear?' she asked.

'Oh, Alice,' Joanna replied. 'I am mortified. We were walking together in the woods when Hugh suddenly grabbed me in his arms and kissed me. I was so surprised that my breath caught in my throat, and I had to push him away as I was coughing and choking. It all seemed so absurd that I burst out laughing, but then he seemed offended. He apologised profusely, but he didn't speak to me again after that and we returned to the castle in silence.'

Alice could not help but laugh. 'Serves him right for taking liberties,' she said.

'He was so careful all along, that's why it was so unexpected,' said Joanna. 'Then he just lunged at me, and I was completely unprepared!'

'You know,' said Alice, 'it wouldn't surprise me if it was the first time Hugh de Montel attempted to kiss a girl.'

'Oh, the poor fellow,' said Joanna, laughing a little.

The next morning at breakfast, the embarrassment clearly persisted. Alice watched as Joanna and Hugh sat stiffly apart, avoiding each other's eyes. Finally, they faced each other. All eyes were on them, and he bowed stiffly and she curtseyed formally. Their eyes darted about, avoiding each other.

'You asked me to suggest a date for our marriage?' Joanna said, gently. 'I thought perhaps a Christmas wedding would be nice?'

Hugh's body relaxed, and he strained to control his emotions before replying. 'Christmas would be perfect,' he said. 'You shall make me the happiest of men.'

'I consider myself the most fortunate of ladies,' said Joanna.

Everyone clapped and the tension between the couple was broken.

To Alice's consternation, once Hugh left, Joanna showed little inclination to prepare for her nuptials. Unlike her niece, Alice was alarmed at how little time a Christmas ceremony would allow for preparations. 'You might have consulted with me first,' she grumbled. 'I've always favoured springtime ceremonies as the natural season for weddings.'

'Who is getting married, Alice, you or I?' Joanna replied.

They'd not spoken directly about it, but they both understood that Alice would accompany Joanna to her new estate and share her new life and, of course, her good fortune.

Alice would never have conceived of not accompanying Joanna, but she felt some sadness of her own at the idea of leaving court and her friend, Marie.

Eleanor suggested that the nuptials be celebrated just after she returned from Chinon, where she would once again spend the festive season with Henry. Like Joanna, she showed no inclination to discuss the preparations, her mind being occupied by more pressing affairs. It seemed that all was not entirely well between Becket and Henry. Becket was insisting on excommunicating those bishops who had colluded with Henry over the coronation of the young king. As archbishop, Becket had the power to carry out his threat to excommunicate three of the most powerful bishops in England. Henry was again beside himself with anger and had to be convinced not to revoke the safe passage he'd granted Becket.

Once again, Eleanor's diplomacy was instrumental in negotiating the situation and at the end of November, the ship carrying the archbishop back to his seat in Canterbury set sail from France. On December 1st, Becket disembarked at Sandwich and rode without incident to Canterbury where he received a warm welcome from clergy and laymen. Only then did Eleanor relax enough to start preparing for the Christmas season — and Joanna's nuptials. Special fabrics were ordered from the silk weavers of Lyon and the dressmaker was employed for days on end.

One morning, Alice and Joanna stood warming their backs by the fire and gazing out at the pristine blanket of snow which had covered everything as they slept. A glittering crescent moon still lingered in a chilly blue sky.

'I'd give a good tooth for another hour in bed,' moaned Alice.

'Not I,' said Joanna. 'I can't wait to get out of doors!'

They were both wearing long woollen dresses, buttoned up the front, only Joanna's was a sleek fawn with a mink collar and Alice's was plain black. They were much preoccupied with preparations for both Joanna's wedding — especially her trousseau — and the royal family's imminent annual trip to Chinon. Due to her upcoming nuptials, Alice and Joanna were to stay behind at Poitiers while the other ladies accompanied Eleanor to Chinon. They were relieved not to have to endure the discomfort of Henry's vast and freezing estate.

'This cold weather gives me quite an appetite,' said Joanna. 'Come, let's go for breakfast.'

Many of Eleanor's ladies had descended before them, busy as they were with preparations for Chinon. Joanna helped herself to two cold pheasant drumsticks while Alice had her usual quails' eggs and ale.

Moments later, Eleanor swept in with Marie by her side. The ladies all rose quickly and bowed — taken by surprise.

'Carry on with your breakfast, ladies.' Eleanor motioned for them to sit.

'You are risen early this morning, my lady,' Joanna ventured. 'Perhaps you are eager, as I am, to be out of doors?'

Eleanor smiled, but her eyes looked strained. She and Marie wore thick, black cloaks over long tunics and heavy boots, almost like mourning costumes.

'We are not risen to enjoy the snow,' Marie said. 'A messenger from Henry's court arrived in the night with unwelcome tidings. It seems that Becket has followed through with his threat to excommunicate the bishops of York, London and Salisbury for colluding with Henry over the young king's coronation. He had the letters of excommunication published without consulting Henry. The archbishop is more popular than ever since resuming his seat, and Henry's hands are tied regarding the excommunications. He will have to tread most carefully to avoid igniting Becket's anger further, but neither can he ignore the fact that Becket is trying to subvert and undermine the King of England. This is a great embarrassment for the Crown. Henry thus sent his messenger to my mother asking for her counsel on the matter.'

'I have sent an envoy to the Pope requesting that he grant the three bishops a pardon,' added Eleanor. 'We are to travel to Paris today in hopes that His holiness will grant us an interview. Afterwards, we shall travel straight back to Chinon to keep Christmas with Henry.'

Alice and Joanna expressed their heartfelt sympathy, for it was clear that Eleanor was upset.

'Let us know if there is anything we can do to assist,' Alice offered.

'Well,' said Eleanor, 'there is one thing. Under these new, trying circumstances, I need to have my most trusted ladies about me. Joanna...' She turned to her. 'Would you mind dreadfully if I asked you to change your plans and travel to keep Christmas in Chinon with us after all? You too, of course, Alice. There'll still be plenty of time for wedding preparations afterwards.'

Joanna and Alice agreed to go at once; their first loyalty was to Eleanor.

After Joanna went out to walk, Alice stole the opportunity to work on the bedspread she was secretly embroidering for Joanna's bridal bed. Whenever she could, she worked away in a linen-closet underneath the stairwell. Today, she took special comfort in the dark, but cosy, confinement, as it was so cold outside. She liked to imagine presenting it to Joanna and sharing in the joy of furnishing her bedchamber with it. She even allowed herself to imagine sewing and embroidering tiny costumes for Joanna's babies and the great pleasure she would derive from making herself useful in that way.

So, they were to go to Chinon after all! Well, at least she would see Marie over the Christmas period. She'd try to be brave and spend as much time as possible with her. Chretien had again been taking up much of Marie's time, but she'd have her to herself over Christmas.

CHAPTER NINETEEN

Eleanor's ladies climbed into the carriage that was to take them to the boat for Chinon. They were a party of six — poor Rosemary had again been left behind. Their baggage was following on an oxcart, and they were in high spirits — in spite of the overcrowding and the bumpy track.

They stopped before the sucking river as light was breaking, and the horses were given water while the ladies sat on their baggage and waited. An eerie horn announced the boat's arrival and they embarked in silence. Alice was jittery in anticipation of her reunion with Marie.

When they arrived, a guard was waiting to escort them straight to the castle. They were brought to the windowless dayroom situated under the stairwell which led to the ladies' bedchamber. There, a breakfast had been spread and Eleanor, Marie and Richard were waiting. After warm embraces, they settled to eat. At once Alice could see that Marie had lost weight and was fatigued. She knew she must have passed a terribly stressful few weeks, for whatever troubles fell on Eleanor's shoulders were shared by Marie.

'You've grown thin,' Alice said, when they had a quiet moment together.

'You've no idea,' Marie said, squeezing her hand and grimacing. 'The Pope blames Henry for acting against the Church and refuses to intervene. Mother has been praying night and day, for she fears some terrible punishment is in store for Henry. I have never seen her so distressed, Alice. She rails against Henry for his rash foolishness in having the young king crowned without the archbishop. I've tried to calm her, telling her that what's done cannot be undone, but she is convinced that God will mete out punishment. I said, "Mother, it is Becket and not God who seeks revenge!" Alice, I fear this is not going to be a merry Christmas.'

After breakfast, Eleanor went to rest and Marie sought out the comforting company of the musicians — taking Joanna with her. Alice, once again, found herself without company or occupation, but quickly quelled her disappointment. What were her troubles compared to their queen's?

Eleanor had joined Henry in his private chambers, so her ladies were free to spend the evening as they wished. Alice went to the great hall on her own. She accepted a goblet of mead and moved close to the fireplace, which acted as a conduit for the howling gale. Groups of gaily dressed ladies were huddled before it, chatting, but she found them neither friendly not inviting. She'd just resolved to return to the bedchamber, when Joanna entered, apparently looking for her.

'Aunt Alice!'

The ladies paused, glancing furtively, clearly surprised that Alice was related to this beautiful girl. She felt a tinge of pride.

'May I?' Joanna drained the goblet. 'I needed that!' She seemed upset. 'Can we go somewhere to talk?'

'Calm yourself, Joanna, dear.'

They sat together on a clumsy, wooden bench and spoke in low voices.

'I shouldn't have come here, Alice.'

'We had to come. Eleanor requested it. What on earth is the matter? Is it Marie? Did something happen?'

'What? No! It's not Marie… It's Jean. He was so cold with me just now. I believe he hates me!'

'Ah.' Alice was relieved. 'Why would Jean hate you?'

'You don't understand. He asked me to marry him and I refused, and now he knows I'm engaged to Hugh de Montel and he hates me.'

Tears rolled down Joanna's cheeks. Alice passed her a linen cloth. She had no experience of such matters.

'He asked you to marry him? When?'

'Yes! Last Christmas. I told no one. Well, apart from Heloise.'

'I see. Well, I'm sure he's just hurt. Don't worry, he'll forgive you. You made the right choice. It's not important in the larger scheme of things. Looks what's happening between the king and Thomas Becket! Look what poor Eleanor and her family are going through. Our troubles are as nothing compared to theirs, you see.'

'No, Alice, I don't see.' Joanna's lips tightened as she frowned. 'My troubles seem every bit as important to me as theirs must seem to them. You are only worried about Marie!'

'Don't speak such nonsense,' Alice said. 'There are real dangers ahead for Eleanor's family that cannot be compared to lovers' quarrels. Grow up, Joanna.'

'I have no sisters or mama to confide in,' Joanna sniffed. 'Jean's friendship means the world to me, for I've been deprived of friendship my whole life. How I crave it, Alice! It's more important to me than a distant archbishop in a distant land with a distant king!'

'I'm certain Jean will understand in time,' Alice said. 'He must see that you could never have married him, for he has no fortune to inherit. Soon you'll be a grand countess, Joanna, with children of your own, and you'll not think of Jean.'

'I'll not give up Jean,' Joanna said, fiercely. 'I'll not lose him. I've already lost too much…'

'Joanna, compose yourself,' said Alice, surprised. 'What are you talking about? You'll not be able to keep a friend like Jean once you're married, you know that.'

'I'll not give him up,' Joanna repeated. 'What would you know of love? I should not have mentioned anything to you, Alice, for you don't understand. Only I was so upset I felt I'd burst if I did not.'

'I understand more than you imagine,' Alice said, sorrowfully. 'I too know the pain of loss ... the fear of further loss. But you must cease this wild talk, Joanna. I thought you'd grown more sensible than this.'

'That's just it.' Joanna was crying again. 'I've not become more sensible. I'm exactly the same as I always was in here.' She pressed her heart. 'I'll always be the same, and my wild talk is the true reflection of my heart. Come, you know it's true.'

Alice considered and yes — she knew. 'It's true,' she said, gently. 'Your nature was always free. I used to fear that your free nature and my strange one would get us into trouble. Only recently have I begun to hope that we will thrive in spite of it. You see, we have survived thus far, against the odds, and now I believe we may continue to survive.'

Joanna nodded. 'We have survived. We have even been favoured.'

'Indeed,' said Alice. 'I was certain that Eleanor would turn us out after your misadventure last summer, but she did not. She sheltered us instead and gave us every opportunity to thrive.'

'She has been our saviour,' said Joanna. 'I see now I've been selfish to concern myself with Jean while Eleanor's family is in peril.'

'That's the spirit,' said Alice. 'Let's dry those eyes and attend our queen.'

By Christmas day, all was in place for a tremendous feast. In the great hall, torches with wicks steeped overnight in nettle and poppy paste were sending bright green and red flames dancing across the stone walls. The ladies held Eleanor's train as she descended in a heavy brocaded gown of purple with gold stars. Her elaborate headdress and the silk, orange veil covering half her face made her look like the new bride of some Turkish sultan. Her feet were shod in skinny gold shoes which curled up dramatically at the ends.

Joanna wore a frothy pale green dress with lace sleeves and the hem cut short enough both for dancing and to show off her footwear. She looked like some divine Grecian nymph in her lagoon dress, little gems sparkling in her loose auburn curls.

Marie and Alice were both in black at Eleanor's righthand side — like matronly guardian angels. Eleanor had requested that they keep close, fearful of Henry's drunken temper. Richard was waiting at the bottom of the stairwell, and he took her hand and kissed it solemnly. Eleanor laid a hand on his arm and let him lead her.

Joanna joined the musicians onstage for the opening recital. Henry arrived soon after with his attending knights. When Richard stood next to his father, the resemblance was striking — though Henry's face was more dissipated and his body bloated with age — his son shared his impressive stature, sea-blue eyes and red hair.

Marie and Alice scarcely dared to speak a word in Henry's presence, and Alice regretted that nerves prevented her from tasting the fine food. At Chinon, each course was introduced by marshals waving wands and followed by a different act on stage. Today being Christmas day, there were many courses, followed by many acts. Henry's rich laughter bellowed around the hall at the clowning-acts he so enjoyed. That all changed when a mime-artist enacted a dispute between a king and an archbishop. The outcome was, of course, flattering to the king, with the archbishop bowing to kiss his ring, but Henry heckled the players angrily.

'Enough of that nonsense, enough!' he shouted. 'Off! Off!'

Eleanor was tense and troubled, and Richard sat as straight and stiff as a bow. Alice and Marie exchanged worried glances — they'd all be glad when the banquet was over.

All the acts competed now and the drumming of instruments, beating of feet, and loud voices echoed round the bare walls of the massive hall to create an almighty din. It might have been a happy, festive party, if it wasn't for Eleanor's constant watchfulness and apprehension, also felt by Richard and her ladies.

The noise prevented them from hearing the banging on the outer door in the small hours of the morning. Many of the guards and knights were by now dulled with drink or asleep and snoring.

A messenger from Canterbury was finally let through with an urgent message: 'From his pulpit in Canterbury this very day, the archbishop Thomas Becket denounced the renegade bishops of York, London and Salisbury, publishing sentence of excommunication on them. Henry King of England is guilty of crowning the young king in the absence of the archbishop, and sentence of excommunication on him is pending a formal apology to the Church for this offense.'

Henry's voice thundered over the noise. 'Who will rid me of this turbulent priest? Clear out! All of you!' The table with all its dishes went flying into the air, crashing mercilessly on the stone flags.

In no time the hall was clear. The messenger was quaking in spite of his exhaustion.

'Quick, ladies.' Eleanor's face was grave and pale. 'Show him to a chamber and then go to the bedchamber and wait for me. Marie, stay with me.' She clutched her daughter's hand. 'Richard...'

'I shall stay, Mother.'

Joanna sat on the bed while Alice paced about with worry.

'Jean and I are speaking again,' Joanna confided. Her eyes were shining.

'Ah, that's good. I told you he'd understand in time.'

'I do love him, Alice.'

'Yes, we love those who offer us friendship.' Alice was scarcely listening, distracted by the commotion in the hall.

'You and the princess are great friends?'

Alice glanced at her sharply, but Joanna's expression was innocent. 'I consider Marie and I to be the best of friends.'

'Then you know the worth of such a friendship,' said Joanna. 'When Mama died, I had no friends and I thought I'd die of loneliness when we first came to court. Now I have two great friends, Heloise and Jean. I mean to keep them forever and ever.'

Alice smiled faintly and patted her shoulder. They'd fallen asleep on the bed — still dressed — by the time Eleanor and Marie returned and woke them.

'She wants you to sleep with us,' Marie whispered, solemnly.

They changed into their nightshifts and went to Eleanor's bedside.

'Come,' Eleanor said to Joanna, pushing back the sheets.

'Alice, this side,' Marie beckoned. Soon they were tucked up all together, one on either side.

Alice was grateful for the warmth emanating from Marie's generous body. She dared not move in case they touched. She breathed in her sweet, honeysuckle perfume and felt herself a carefree child again, at play in a meadow, before all the suffering and loss. The scent of honeysuckle would forever after evoke in her a sense of peace.

In her sleep, Eleanor muttered, sometimes crying out. 'Richard! Becket! Oh God... Mercy.'

'Hush, Mother, hush,' Marie soothed. Joanna also whispered words of comfort, but Alice never knew the right thing to say so she just lay there, so still and scarcely breathing, but happy.

To Alice's surprise, she slept and woke to hear the ladies speaking low among themselves. Eleanor was complaining of a headache, and Marie massaged her temples while Joanna rubbed lavender into the soles of her feet. Lines were visible for once around Eleanor's eyes, and her forehead was stuck in a frown. Marie's sallow skin looked ashen, and her eyes were sunk in dark sockets. Alice felt their anxiety and wished that she could help.

'Is there anything I can do?' she asked.

'Just stay close to us over the coming days,' Eleanor replied. 'We are most worried. Last night, after Henry had exhausted himself with his rant, one of his knights crept in to inform us that four of his knights had decided to take matters into their own hands and had ridden out with the intention of crossing for England and riding to Canterbury.'

'And what are their intentions once they get there?'

'That's what frightens us the most,' explained Marie. 'You remember when Henry shouted, "Who will rid me of this turbulent priest?"? Henry is afraid his knights took his words literally and mean to harm Becket in some way. Of course,

Henry says all kinds of dreadful things when he's in a rage, but he doesn't mean them. Henry loved Becket once; he'd love him still if only this quarrel was resolved once and for all.'

Eleanor groaned. 'The trouble with Henry is he loves us all to death,' she said. 'He generously bestows positions of power and influence on those he loves and afterwards he tries to tie their hands — taking away the very gift he bestowed. He does not seem to realise that he's doing it; he believes it's for the common good. He trusts no one but himself. He loved Becket's intelligence and charisma and so he made him Archbishop of Canterbury. But he expected Becket to do his will. However, the very intelligence and charm that Henry loved in Becket makes it impossible for him to be anyone's pawn.'

'Do not tire yourself, Mother,' advised Marie. 'Perhaps this will teach Henry a valuable lesson and he'll no longer let such intemperate words fly from his mouth.'

'Filthy words,' said Eleanor. 'May God forgive him. Ladies, we must rise, for it's growing light. We must find out if the knights have been discovered. Last night,' she explained, 'Henry sent some men-at-arms in pursuit to summon back his knights at his behest. I hope they managed to catch up with them before they made the crossing.'

Eleanor splashed rosewater on her face and stepped out of her nightgown into a dark wool dress. Alice tied all the little buttons while Marie summoned her maid, Amaria, to dress Eleanor's hair and make up her face. They descended together, skipping breakfast to go straight to the great hall.

The grim faces of Henry's attending-knights and the sound of raised voices from the hall made clear all was not well. Eleanor paused, bracing herself before entering, with Marie on one side and Joanna and Alice on the other.

They were amazed to find the spectacle of three bishops in impressive robes. For a second, Alice thought the elaborate garbs were costumes and they were another of Henry's acts. However, their serious countenances announced exactly who they were — as well as the city colours on their seals and staffs — they were the excommunicated bishops of York, Salisbury and London, come to make their complaint.

Henry was seated on his throne, looking down in stony silence as they railed venomously against Becket. Eleanor stepped up to take her seat beside Henry. When the bishops finally paused, it was she — and not Henry — who spoke.

'Forgive us, Your Holinesses, but don't the bishops take their orders from the archbishop, not the king? Doesn't the king take his orders from the Pope? Has not the Pope declared that the archbishop's sentence of excommunication be observed? Therefore, it is not possible for us to reverse this sentence at the present time. At a later time it will, perhaps, be possible to reverse the sentence, but we must be patient.'

The bishops clearly did not like Eleanor, and they hated being addressed by her. They did not look at her as she spoke, and they replied to Henry as if it were he who had spoken.

The disgruntled bishops departed with the Crown's promise of support and reassurance of a future reinstatement of their titles — if possible.

Eleanor stepped down and departed with her ladies without uttering a word to Henry. The four knights had not been located.

'It is Henry's character, I believe, that has led to all this trouble,' Eleanor seethed.

CHAPTER TWENTY

The chapel at Chinon was as primitive as the rest of the castle, but it was here that Eleanor spent the most part of the coming days — in a stone building no warmer than an outhouse. Dressed in her plainest clothes, with a veil covering her face, she asked her ladies to pray with her.

'Pray that fierce guardian angels watch over and protect the soul of Thomas Becket,' she said. 'I have a terrible feeling about this.'

The morning of December 31st, a messenger arrived with the worst news: Thomas Becket had been murdered in Canterbury Cathedral.

The traumatised messenger recounted the horrific details of the murder with tears streaming down his face. Alice and the other ladies listened in shock. The outcome that Eleanor had feared and expected most had come to pass, even if she had attempted to ward it off with prayers.

'Evil wins out,' Eleanor muttered, making multiple signs of the cross.

The messenger had received his information from an eyewitness named Edward Grim, one of the monks who was by Becket's side as the murder took place. The four knights, Reginald FitzUrse, William de Tracy, Hugh de Morville and Richard de Brito had first confronted Becket in his study in Canterbury, threatening him with terrible consequences if he did not agree to leave England. The messenger's hands were shaking uncontrollably as he unrolled the parchment and read the monk's account: 'When the monks went in procession to Canterbury Cathedral that evening for vespers, the knights followed them with rapid strides. When the holy Archbishop entered the Church, the monks stopped vespers and ran to him, glorifying God that they saw their father.

'When they saw the knights approaching with their swords drawn the monks bolted the doors to the church, to protect their shepherd from the slaughter. But Becket ordered the church doors to be thrown open, saying, "It is not meet to make a fortress of the house of prayer, the church of Christ." And straightaway the knights entered the house of prayer with swords sacrilegiously drawn, causing horror to the beholders with their very looks and the clanging of their arms.'

Alice gasped, certain that Becket — like any hunted animal — had known his death was approaching.

'"Absolve and restore to communion those whom you have excommunicated!" they demanded. Becket said he would not. "Then you shall die!" was the reply. "I am ready to die for my Lord, that in my blood the Church may find liberty and peace." Then they laid their sacrilegious hands on him, pulling him and dragging him that they might kill him outside the church.'

The monk's account ended there, but the messenger, tears spilling down his cheeks, described how all of the monks had abandoned Becket to his fate, apart from Grim. Miraculously, Grim had lived to tell the tale, despite almost having his arm sliced off by FitzUrse's sword as he tried to defend Becket.

Eleanor had to be supported to her seat, while the messenger was given strong, sweetened wine. Richard entered and ran to embrace his mother. The ladies stood back as mother and son sobbed in each other's arms. After some time, they were calm enough to speak.

'You must go to your father, Richard, for I cannot bear to look upon his wretched face.'

'I've already seen him, Mama. He is weeping so copiously I fear that no one has ever suffered such deep grief.'

'Henry loved Thomas, but no one will believe it. No one will suffer the consequences of this murder more than he,' said Eleanor. 'All of Christendom knew of their feud and all will believe that Henry ordered his knights to murder Thomas.'

'Yet no one could be sorrier than he,' sighed Richard. 'He means to abuse himself for this evil act.'

'Truly this is the most tragic murder of an innocent since the time of Christ Our Lord,' said Eleanor.

Over the coming days, Henry kept to his chamber where it was said he practised self-flagellation and wore a painful hairshirt under his clothes, refusing all meals.

'So much the better,' said Eleanor, 'for I cannot bear to set eyes on him. May God forgive him for what he has done. Ah, poor Becket!' She spent much time in prayer and sent Richard and Marie to preside over the evening banquet in her place.

The day before their departure for Poitiers, Eleanor called Alice and Joanna to her.

'My dear Joanna,' she said. 'Forgive us in our time of mourning, but we must act with great decorum and therefore we cannot allow your wedding to take place until a future time.'

Alice was surprised to see that Joanna seemed relieved.

News of Becket's murder preceded their arrival back in Poitiers, and they were met by a subdued and fearful court.

'Thank heavens I was not there,' said a tearful Rosemary. 'I'd not for all the world be implicated in such a foul affair. As an English lady born and bred, I must say I'm appalled!'

'We are all of us appalled,' snapped Joanna. 'Eleanor is certainly not implicated, and neither are her ladies. Even Henry is implicated only by default of his knights. It is a tragedy of huge proportions.'

Before leaving Chinon, Eleanor's final task had been to arrange for envoys to be sent to Pope Alexander to verify that Henry had not — contrary to common opinion — ordered Becket's murder. The knights had acted autonomously, and no one was more horrified than Henry at the outcome.

She had, however, refused to see Henry before she left, claiming that she was repulsed by the part that he had played — even if he was innocent of the actual bloodshed. From now on, she had told her ladies, she would distance herself and her children from Henry and his policies. She knew that Henry's name would be forever sullied for his part in Becket's murder.

CHAPTER TWENTY-ONE

After Becket's murder, the faithful had rushed to Canterbury to fill vials of his blood or to take snippets from his vestments. By Easter, rumours of miracles taking place at his tomb were widespread. It appeared that Becket dead was more powerful than Becket alive. Henry remained in self-imposed solitary confinement as he awaited judgment from the Pope, but the four knights who had committed the atrocity were excommunicated and exiled to a remote castle in Yorkshire. The fact that Henry had not punished them himself led to more speculation over his guilt.

In Poitiers, however, life went back to normal as Easter Sunday celebrations were underway. Eleanor's spirits had revived and she threw herself into her favourite pursuits of hawking and music, with Joanna often by her side. The warm weather and longer days drew the whole court outside.

After a prolonged mass with sacred music, at which Eleanor wept and lit candles for Becket, banqueting tables had been set out in the sun and the mouth-watering aroma of roasting lamb on spits wafted through the air. Eleanor had proposed a fancy dress with an Eastern theme and she and the younger ladies in her retinue dressed in belly-dancing costumes, with bulbous pants and midriff-revealing bodices. Each wore a glittering jewel between their eyes, which were painted thick with coal. Bowls of delicate snails in herb-infused wine were passed about to whet the appetite and the musicians struck up a jubilant tune on pipe and tabor. Alice watched as Joanna began dancing on the green in her ornate costume, her bracelets jingling with each turn. All eyes were fixed on her, despite the fact that others too were dancing. People began clapping and as the music grew more frenzied, so too did Joanna's steps, until she was whirling round as light as air. Alice saw Hugh de Montel walk over to Joanna and grab her by the arm.

'Hugh!' Joanna gasped. 'I didn't know you were here! Is something wrong?'

'Would you have been dancing like that had you known I was in the crowd?' Hugh said, angrily.

Joanna tried to cover her midriff with her hands. 'It is a fancy dress,' she said, miserably. 'I was only dancing.'

Alice saw Bertran de Born hovering near the couple as she listened uneasily to their conversation.

'We must talk,' Hugh said. 'I've heard some rumours, Joanna … about you.'

'What have you heard and from whom did you hear it?' Joanna's voice was now raised.

'From the troubadour, Bertran de Born, if you must know.'

'You know very well that I slighted Bertran de Born and he has hated me ever since!'

'Yes, I know. That's why I challenged him to prove his allegations or else meet with the end of my sword.' Hugh drew out a parchment and Alice saw Joanna grow pale. 'This was intercepted by de Born's men and passed to me. It has your signature, Joanna. You cannot deny it was written by your hand?'

'There is nothing in that note that is reprehensible,' Joanna said. 'I don't deny I wrote it, but Jean and I are merely friends.'

'Bertran says that you and he are more than friends. But even so, you have used a tone of intimacy with him that you don't even use with me. It's not seemly for a lady to write like this to a man of no relation.'

'Not seemly, not seemly!' Joanna cried. 'I care not a fiddlestick for what's seemly. What I do care for are my friends. I thought you were one of them, Hugh, but I see that I was wrong. I cannot believe you'd listen to anything Bertran de Born would say concerning me. Can't you see he's jealous because he couldn't have me and wishes to split us up?'

'Joanna.' Hugh looked apologetic. 'I thought you were chaste and now I am not sure. I only ask that you are honest with me.'

'This lady is not chaste,' Bertran said, approaching. 'She has been seen with Jean.'

'Why are you doing this?' Joanna hissed.

'Because, Lady, you broke my heart and cared not a whit for my feelings, and now I have the opportunity to take my revenge. Apart from that, I believe this knight has the right to know your true character which you've so artfully concealed from him. I've watched you string him along while conducting your affair, and I don't believe you deserve his love ... nor his estate and title. You claimed you would not marry me on grounds of immorality, but your behaviour is no better than mine and your vanity, Lady, is unparalleled even by my own.'

'Bertran!' It was the queen. 'Hugh de Montel. How dare you accuse Lady Joanna in such a manner on this day of celebration. Whatever she has or has not done, she is not yet married and has committed no crime. Come away, Joanna, they are unworthy of your attentions.'

Joanna ran crying to her bedchamber with Alice close behind.

'Oh, my poor girl,' said Alice. 'I heard the dreadful accusations Bertran made. Everyone knows that he is acting out of jealousy and spite! Don't worry, it is just a lover's tiff that will soon blow over.'

'Alice, it's true. I am not chaste. I have had ... relations with Jean.'

Alice stared at her, then sat down. She was shocked and angry with herself for not keeping a closer watch on her niece. She knew Joanna had grown up fast, but she could not believe that her young ward had deceived her and been intimate with Jean.

'He'll not have me now, I'm sure, and I'll soon be an old maid,' Joanna wailed.

Alice almost smiled despite herself. 'Then we shall be old maids together.'

'I asked you if you believed I should tell Hugh about myself and you said no, Alice.'

'That's right,' Alice sighed, 'but then I didn't know you'd been intimate with Jean. Now I've no idea what to advise.'

'I don't wish to discuss it any further. I'm going out,' Joanna said, rushing to the door.

'Where are you going?'

'To the forest.'

It was dark when Joanna returned, her face tearstained and pale and her fine dress torn and muddied.

'You're a sight to hurt the eye,' said Alice, angrily. 'Don't ever, ever go out riding alone like that again, Joanna, or I swear I'll disown you.'

'You hate me now!' Joanna wailed.

'Not so,' said Alice, softening. 'I understand the temptations of the flesh, and you are young and ... I could never hate you, Joanna. I am not as angry as you believe over your indiscretion with Jean... This may in fact blow over quickly like a summer storm. Morals are looser in this part of the world and few young ladies remain chaste for long, especially at court.'

'I wish I'd not been born so beautiful,' said Joanna, 'for it seems to have caused nothing but grief!'

'Would you rather have been born ugly like me? Your beauty is a gift from God, the same as any other gift. Be grateful for it, but don't abuse it.'

Alice wanted to comfort Joanna, but could not help feeling that her niece had let them both down. She was again assaulted by the old fear that Joanna's free nature and her own strange one would be their downfall.

CHAPTER TWENTY-TWO

King Henry was absolved of all guilt in relation to Becket's murder and on Richard's 15th birthday, Eleanor and Henry agreed that he was old enough to be made Duke of Aquitaine. Eleanor would not relinquish her title, but mother and son would rule the Duchy together. As Count, Richard proved himself to be a reliable and natural leader and — unlike his brother — he was thrifty. While his brother excelled at games and tournaments, he showed a greater aptitude for hunting and hawking. In fact, he seemed to emulate his mother in most things, being an avid patron of troubadour poetry and a true child of the South. He was blessed with his half-sister, Marie, who helped nurture his talents, and he spent long hours composing with Marie and Chretien.

With only eleven days before his investiture as Duke, the court was buzzing with excitement. No expense would be spared, and a period of lavish feasting and entertainment was planned to follow the ceremony. Eleanor had invited many troubadours and gentle lyrics and laughter could be heard resounding round the Tower at all hours.

During this period, Hugh de Montel tentatively resumed his visits. He had decided not to believe the rumours spread by Bertran, and Joanna had no intention of confessing the truth. She spent much time out hawking with the queen and in her absence, Alice had seized the opportunity to work on her bridal bedspread. She'd settled herself comfortably in the secret closet with a stool and candle. She surveyed her handiwork with pride, for it was really beautiful and special, a labour of love; it depicted Joanna's various pursuits in colourful embroidery. That morning she'd been working on a forest scene, with Joanna in hunting garb surrounded by trees and animals, hawks circling overhead. She realised she was out of gold thread for the foxes and stepping out with her candle, she bumped into Marie under the stairwell.

'My goodness,' Marie exclaimed, 'what were you doing in there?'

Alice, blushing foolishly, had to confide her secret. 'Come, let me show you,' she said.

Intrigued, Marie followed her into the closet. 'I don't believe I've ever been in here!' she said, amused. 'What is it, a broom closet?'

'It's for storing linens and blankets, so it's quite warm,' said Alice. 'You can sit there, if you like.'

Marie's dark eyes were round with curiosity, and her features looked soft and younger in the candlelight. Alice's heart filled with so much tenderness that she almost reached for Marie's hand.

'Would you mind holding this side?' Alice gave Marie one end and slowly rolled it out. 'It's a surprise for Joanna's wedding and a means of passing the time when I am alone.'

Marie held the candle close to survey it. 'Alice, it's wonderful,' she said in awe. 'You are an artist, truly! I am not surprised, for I've always said you were a lady of the finest sensibility and depth.'

Alice was so touched that tears came to her eyes and she was rendered speechless. She didn't think anyone would find her worthy of anything but disdain, yet here she was receiving such praise from a princess! Not just any princess, one she revered more than anyone in the world.

They heard footsteps in the corridor and hurriedly left the closet, Alice stashing the bedspread in its hiding place.

That was the last time Alice was alone with Marie for some time, as she was preoccupied with Richard and the troubadours. Alice spent most of her time in the bedchamber, sheltering from the sun and the noisy entertainers. She felt as bleak as a desert inside and wondered how Marie could forget her so easily. Marie seemed flattered by Richard's attentions — which Alice failed to understand — and she continued to seek out Chretien's intelligent company. Alice felt dull and withered, like a flower deprived of sunlight. After another friendless day, she was feeling lethargic and downcast when Joanna entered in her bright, carefree way.

'I don't know which I love more,' Joanna declared. 'Hawking or performing!' She flung her music down carelessly.

'Careful,' Alice scolded.

'Today I should say I love performing most! I just received the nicest praise!'

'Really, Joanna, you should not scatter your papers about so...'

Joanna sat at the glass and shook out her hair. 'It was such a marvellous day, Alice,' she continued. 'You should have heard us! Richard has a fine voice and we performed Eleanor's new Tenso together. I suppose you were with Chretien and Marie? What is this narrative they're preparing they're being so secretive about?'

Alice was lanced through with hurt; why had they not asked her to join them as before? Probably because she couldn't read or write and they were too intelligent for her. They'd found her out and cast her aside as she'd feared.

'Ha! You are as mysterious as they!' said Joanna, mistaking her silence for secrecy. She stretched happily. 'I must hurry and change before the banquet. My goodness, how late is the day? We were having too much fun to notice the time passing! Have you ever thought, Alice, how you would miss court life? I would miss it dreadfully, especially at happy times like this!'

'I'd not miss it at all,' said Alice curtly. She watched Joanna admiring herself in the glass and thought how right Bertran was when he called her vain. 'Have you and Hugh spoken about your wedding of late?' she asked abruptly.

Joanna's mouth curled with displeasure. 'We have not. There's been so much to divert, and everyone is preoccupied with Richard's investiture.'

'There's always some excuse,' said Alice. 'I advise you to set a date, Joanna, before it's too late. He'll tire of waiting and choose another to keep his bed warm next winter.'

Joanna swung around. 'And then what, Alice? You and I are whisked away to Hugh's estate? You'd like that, wouldn't you? I'll not provide a cave for you to hide in. That is not my purpose.'

Alice blinked back angry tears. 'Don't you dare speak to me like that. Go back to your games, Joanna,' she said quietly. 'That is your only purpose, as far as I can see. At least I do not hurt others with my vanity.'

'I'll not do it. I'll NOT be forced into marriage by anyone.' Joanna ran from the room, leaving Alice upset and confused.

On the 11th of June, in the abbey of Saint-Martial in Limoges, Richard received the ring of St Valerie and was proclaimed Duke of Aquitaine. At fifteen, he already towered over Eleanor and he looked serious and thoughtful in his green silk tunic and gold coronet. The people lit bonfires all the way from Limoges to Poitiers and a national holiday was declared, for Richard's investiture imbued them with fresh hope. Many of the barons had a fractious relationship with Henry, and they recognised Richard as one of their own kind — a child of the

South with southern sentiments.

The monks lit candles and chanted in complex polyphony as the thurible was swung heavily over and back, filling the air with incense. Eleanor knelt to kiss her son's ring and the Church fell silent.

Alice looked over to where Joanna, Rosemary and Hugh were standing. Joanna's purple and orange stripes hugged her gorgeous, youthful form; Hugh's yellow tunic was brocaded with gold and Rosemary looked willowy in her lemon silk dress to match her yellow hair. Joanna had avoided Alice since their argument, but Alice stared in shock as she saw Hugh and Rosemary were holding hands and he was whispering in her ear. She saw Joanna turn towards them and Hugh quickly withdraw his hand. Joanna gasped and began to push through the crowd towards Alice.

'Joanna! Wait!' Hugh followed her, eventually caught up and grabbed her arm.

'Unhand me!'

'Please, Joanna! Let us speak.'

'No, Hugh, you betrayed my trust.'

'No, Joanna, it is you who betrayed my trust. You were not honest with me. About Jean ... and about what occurred between yourself and Prince Henry.'

Joanna stared at him.

'Rosemary told me.'

'That sneaking harlot.'

'Do not speak of her like that,' Hugh said, sternly. 'You know quite well she is more chaste than you.'

Joanna shrugged. 'What of it? Do you love her? What of our engagement?'

'Had I believed your heart was truly mine, I never would have... I'd even have forgiven your past indiscretions, had I

181

believed you loved me. My heart only turned from yours after I realised that yours did not belong to me.' His tone became gentler. 'Please don't be angry with Rosemary. She insisted that I speak with you first, before…'

'Typical Rosemary, let me guess, she wouldn't let you kiss her until you'd broken our engagement? I must admit, you two are ideally suited. You're both so good and … seemly.' Joanna screwed up her nose. 'She'll be content to live a quiet life on your estate as your perfect wife.'

Hugh smiled. 'We are ideally suited, as you say.'

'To think that it was I who threw the two of you together. Bertran will be sorry to lose her, I suppose.'

'They had no relations,' said Hugh, defensively. 'Joanna, I apologise for being curt, but do you release me from our engagement?'

'I release you from our engagement.'

'Please take my place in the carriage, it is waiting.'

'I'll not travel with her,' Joanna said, nodding to Rosemary.

'I understand. Will you travel with your aunt? It's too wild for you to go about alone.'

Joanna wept the whole way back to Poitiers. Alice suspected they were tears of rage rather than true heartbreak. She wondered if her niece was as ill-fated in love as she herself had been. As Carole had also been. Perhaps they were cursed.

'Well, you were right, Alice,' Joanna gulped. 'He has found someone else to warm his bed this winter. It's all my fault for procrastinating. Now what are we to do? That Rosemary is a sneaking cow, pretending to be my friend when all along she had her eye on Hugh…'

'And Hugh de Montel is blameless, I suppose?'

'He is even worse, but she was supposed to be my friend…'

Alice was silent, unable to offer comfort. Clearly Joanna was in shock, but that would pass and she'd see things more clearly. Alice had begun to suspect that Joanna's feelings for Jean ran deeper then she'd pretended. She thought ruefully — a bit angrily — about the bedspread lovingly crafted in the secret closet. Beautiful and gifted though she was, Joanna would not be an attractive prospect with a string of broken engagements to her name — as well as a rumoured affair.

Back in Poitiers, Alice rushed Joanna through the throngs of gathered courtiers to their bedchamber and helped to tidy her hair and dress for the evening banquet, which they had to attend in spite of all the drama.

Paler than usual, but lovely as always, Joanna managed to perform her duet with Richard to great applause. After, she sat quietly with Alice until the tables were cleared away.

'Please tell Eleanor I have a headache if she is seeking me,' she said, rising.

Having just spent one of the loneliest periods in her life, Alice couldn't muster up enough sympathy to join her, but simply nodded her head.

She found herself unusually drawn into the entertainment. Tiered candle holders had been placed all over the stage, which gave the troubadours and their compositions a mysterious, almost holy light and calmness. Alice watched them, mesmerized with the rest, until she was startled out of her dream-state by a change of scene in preparation for Chretien's narrative. With a mixture of jealousy and curiosity, Alice realised that this must be the secret narrative Joanna had referred to.

It was an interpretation of one of the prophesies of Merlin — always a favourite with the king and queen. A robust player, with painted feathers and the hooked beak of an eagle — red hair beneath the crown on his head to mark him as King Henry — made surprisingly agile, static movements across the stage to discordant strains of music. The eagle-king swept about his forest-kingdom until the music changed, becoming more harmonious, as four graceful eagle-princes emerged, making marvellous acrobatics together — and falling apart as they 'claimed' their land. Two wore coronets over red hair, supposed to depict the princes Henry and Richard, while two wore gold circlets over dark hair — their younger brothers, Geoffrey and John. The eagle-king began to challenge them, with the music becoming again discordant, sweeping across them, attempting to 'rein-in' his young with gold cord. With artful movements, the eagle-princes worked together to free each other and bind their father in the golden cord. Their success was accompanied by heavenly background music.

It was spellbinding and held everyone on the edge of their benches, highly pleasing as it was to both eye and ear. The message was startlingly clear. Eleanor was sitting back surveying her courtiers, her hands together as if in prayer, her expression serious. Alice realised she must have directed the act.

Treason. The word rustled through Alice as wind through dry leaves. She closed her eyes, realised what troubles lay ahead.

'Alice?' It was Marie.

Alice was so relieved she grabbed her hands in hers. 'I thought you had forgotten me!'

'Oh, Alice, I do apologise. Mother made Chretien and I swear secrecy! What did you think?'

'It was very beautiful … and powerful … and shocking.'

Marie's voice lowered to a whisper. 'I found it so as well, strange and disturbing, though beautiful. It is Mother's vision,

Alice, of the future for her sons. I am afraid of what lies ahead for all of us.'

'Hugh de Montel has broken his engagement to Joanna,' Alice blurted out, the atmosphere being conducive to disclosures. 'It's not yet common knowledge.'

'Oh, Alice, I am sorry. What are you going to do?'

'I have no idea… Her father would certainly beat her if he knew the trouble she was causing. Of course, I shall not inform him, though I wish some authority had forced her to marry. I have failed most dreadfully at the task.'

'I know it's selfish of me to say, but I'm really glad we are not to lose the two of you just yet.'

'Could I make a request?' Alice asked. 'Would you speak to Joanna for me? She's not forthcoming with me, for I'm just an old crone in her eyes with no experience of men. Would you attempt to discover if her intentions are serious regarding this musician, Jean?'

'I'll do my best.'

CHAPTER TWENTY-THREE

One dark afternoon in November, Eleanor was sewing lavender pouches with her ladies in the Tower when Richard burst in. Since becoming joint-ruler of the Duchy, he'd grown increasingly aware of — and concerned with — his father's interference with their barons.

'Mother, Baron de Cehl accosted me this morning, complaining that Father had sent him a letter demanding that he cut taxes for his serfs and pay dues out of his own treasury! What business is it of Father's? Does he not trust me to deal with these matters?'

Eleanor frowned and laid down her handiwork. 'No, Richard, he does not. Your father trusts no one but himself. He must believe the rest of us are incompetent, even though we've proven otherwise again and again…'

'The baron raged at me thus, "Sir Richard, is it not enough for you that I pay my dues regularly and by the appointed date? Must you also question the means by which I pay? For what purpose were you crowned if your father still rules the duchy?"' Richard sat heavily, his head in his hands.

Eleanor went to comfort him, her velvet gown sweeping after her.

'What do I tell him, Mama, the Baron de Cehl, or any other baron whom Henry has challenged? Do I have to say our hands are tied?'

'Yes, Richard, our hands are tied. Believe me, it makes me so angry I could scream, but I hope we will be stronger together, you and I, than when I ruled alone. Your brother suffers even worse humiliations, since Henry absolutely refuses to grant him any autonomy even though he has been crowned.'

'I don't envy him his grand title,' said Richard, grimly. 'For though he is the eldest and the heir, he has no land to rule.'

'Precisely,' Eleanor agreed. 'At least we have Poitou, Richard, even if Henry limits our capacities. Your brother agrees that your father is even more savagely autocratic since he was crowned. Louis and I had hoped that our children — Marguerite and Henry — might be granted a kingdom to match their titles, but Henry's grip is as strong as ever and he is unrelenting.'

'The situation is intolerable,' muttered Richard. 'Something must be done.'

'I agree. Louis is determined that his daughter and son-in-law be granted their own kingdom. He wrote to say he has invited your brother and Marguerite for a family gathering. He is going to advise them to demand they be given either England, Normandy or Anjou. Your brother's title is meaningless unless he has some autonomy; therefore, Henry must be forced to loosen his grip.' She placed her dainty, heavily ringed hands on his shoulders and spoke softly. 'With Louis' support, we should be able to weaken Henry's stronghold and strengthen our position so we are not left powerless in our own duchy.'

'It cannot happen soon enough, I say. In the meantime, we'll have to find a way to appease those barons whom Father has insulted.'

'I was thinking,' mused Eleanor. 'You've worked so hard since your investiture this summer. Why not take some rest? You could go to Paris in my stead and discuss the situation with your brothers. I shall encourage your brother Geoffrey to travel also, for he is old enough now to travel alone — and to be granted some land of his own. Then both of you can join us to keep Christmas in Chinon. You may seek advice from Louis, for he is an experienced politician. You know, if Henry can be persuaded to grant a kingdom to your brother, then he ought likewise to be persuaded to give us autonomy finally over Aquitaine. What say you?'

Richard's expression brightened instantly. 'Yes, Mama, I'd like very much to go to Paris and spend time with my brothers.'

'Wonderful! Then it is decided.'

The last week in November, Richard left for Paris as Eleanor and her ladies prepared to depart for Chinon. Rosemary had married Hugh de Montel in September, and Joanna found herself facing another winter alone. The levity that usually surrounded preparations for Chinon was missing this year, and Joanna was the only one pleased to be traveling. Eleanor was jittery from morning till night, making all her ladies anxious too, as she awaited news from Paris. Even Marie was strangely serious, shutting herself away with Chretien and avoiding her mother.

Alice was sleeping poorly and, when she did, she had terrible nightmares. Night or day she couldn't shake the horrible feeling in her body nor the turbulent thoughts in her brain. The uncertainty of their future was like a black cloud drawing down, and she'd no one to seek comfort or advice from as everyone had troubles of their own. More than once she'd attempted to engage Marie, but she'd been too distracted. Never had she felt like such a victim of the self-serving environment of the court. Marie had questioned Joanna some time ago about Jean and discovered that she had deep feelings for him, yet, when Alice requested that they stay behind from Chinon so the relationship might fizzle out, Marie had dismissed her curtly. Alice was deeply offended, especially as she'd lent her own arm so many times for Marie to lean on. To add to her resentment, Joanna was flitting about happily, trying on various gowns as if life was a festival. She seemed oblivious to the sense of impending doom around her.

The night before their departure for Chinon, as she undressed for bed, Joanna was curling her hair, humming to herself.

'Have you had news of Lady Rosemary?' Alice asked.

Joanna cocked her head. 'No. Have you?'

'Only that she is with child, and they are very happy.'

Joanna frowned. 'I'm happy for them.'

'Well, it could have been you.'

'You know, Alice, I'm not sorry. If I was with child and living far from court, I'd miss out on all of … this!' She gestured to her packed trunk.

'Is all of … this so important?'

'Well, yes! Think of the adventures we would miss!'

'I'd happily miss the adventures, Joanna, in exchange for a quiet life.'

'But then you are not really living,' Joanna argued.

'Yes, I am, only in a different kind of way.'

Joanna considered this. 'I'm sorry, Alice,' she said, suddenly. 'I know you wished for me to marry Hugh. I know I have disappointed you… I never meant to, but I couldn't help it.'

Alice said nothing, but she was grateful for the apology.

Joanna was clearly delighted when she set eyes on Jean upon their arrival in Chinon. Alice watched them closely, deeply dismayed at his frayed clothing and his long, tangled hair. Helplessly, she watched them disappearing into the kitchen cellars and guessed what they were up to from Joanna's flushed appearance when she reappeared. These visits were frequent and even the servants would wink and smirk as they emerged, causing great shame to Alice. In desperation, she'd thought of writing to her father to come and reprimand her, but she decided against it. How could she invoke his wrath after all the effort taken to escape it?

Meanwhile, Eleanor and Marie remained aloof and unapproachable as they waited for Richard's arrival from Paris. It didn't help that this winter was the wettest they'd ever experienced at Chinon, with a cold dampness which crept in under the clothes, right through to the very bones. Alice sat with her feet practically in the ashes until her hair and cloak stank unpleasantly of smoke. While Alice shivered constantly, Joanna was flushed with the warmth of her illicit activities.

On the 22nd of December, Henry arrived and Eleanor — dressed in her finest — gathered her ladies round to greet him formally. Alice was shocked by the change in his appearance. In just a few short years he'd gone from vigorous middle-age to elderly, with his rustic beard turned white and his formerly rotund belly sadly deflated. Perhaps the rumours of his diminished power were true. Perhaps he was grown feeble and wished for the young king to rule in his stead. Alice felt a wave of sympathy for him as he greeted his wife lovingly, planting numerous kisses on the cheek she offered. He stood awkwardly and, remembering, he called, 'I have brought gifts for you, most esteemed lady!'

Three knights came forward with delicate caskets. The ladies leaned forward, eagerly, but Eleanor waved them away.

'Our thanks, esteemed husband, but let us first offer you and your men refreshment after your long journey.'

Alice registered the disappointment on his face.

'Very well, my worthy queen, as you wish.'

Henry and his men went to his favourite hall, where a heavy feast was served with extra fortified wine. Eleanor withdrew with her ladies, promising to see him at the evening banquet.

'Take Our Lord's gifts to the monastery as an offering for the soul of Thomas Becket,' she told one of her maids.

'Are you not even going to view them first, Mother?' asked Marie, surprised.

'What for? The gilding is rotten with guilt and the rubies sodden with the blood of the martyr. I shall not contaminate my ladies' chamber with them. Let the monks dispose of them as they wish; they'll know whence they came.'

As Eleanor had intended, Henry did not emerge again following the effects of the potent lunch after a tiring journey. Eleanor and her ladies therefore enjoyed a peaceful evening and retired early in order to be refreshed for the arrival of her sons the next day.

In the bedchamber, they worked together to refresh Eleanor's bed — Marie and Alice on one side, Eleanor and Joanna on the other — spreading the new linens evenly over the lumpy woollen blanket covering the straw mattress.

'Did you see Henry's face when you refused to accept his gifts?' Marie chuckled. 'A brave act, Mother. I thought he might grow angry.'

Eleanor was solemn. 'I did not mean to challenge him,' she sighed, 'but I cannot find it in my heart to forgive him. Accepting his offerings would signify that all is forgiven ... Becket forgotten.'

'Of course.'

'It's pitiful to say, but I am so gagged into silence on these matters that these small gestures are my only means of expression. I'd not dare to challenge or attempt to contradict him openly.'

'You couldn't.'

Alice's fingers were sweaty with nerves, and she wiped them secretly on the sheets.

'I loved the idea of serving the men strong wine so they would sleep!' said Joanna, winking. 'Brilliant!'

Eleanor indulged in a little smile. 'I need some respite before my sons arrive.'

They pulled the heavy fleeces back over the linens and attempted to fluff up the straw pillows before encasing them in felt, brought with them from Poitiers, as a welcome extra comfort.

A knock on the door proved to be Eleanor's maid returned from the monastery. She curtseyed to Eleanor and Marie and nodded to Joanna and Alice.

'Amaria, come sit with us,' Eleanor commanded.

Amaria chose a stool in the far corner, arranging her skirt to cover her muddy boots and placing her hands downward on each lap.

'I trust you delivered our gift safely to the good monks?'

'Yes, my lady. The gifts were delivered safely and were gratefully received.'

'Very good.'

They all stared at her a moment, waiting for her to elaborate, until Marie broke the silence, impatient. 'Well, did the monks open them in your presence?'

'Yes, my lady. They opened them while I took refreshment and exclaimed over each one.'

'Do tell us what they contained!'

'If my memory serves me correctly, the first contained peacocks' feathers coated in gold.'

'Marvellous!' Marie clapped her hands together.

'The second contained seven pearls embedded in their oysters.'

'Oh, my,' Marie uttered, regretfully. 'Such riches gained and lost!'

Eleanor looked at her sternly.

Marie ignored her. 'The third? What was contained in the third?'

'The third contained a camel hair cloak with a red silk lining.'

'What are the monks to do with that?' Marie tittered.

Eleanor rose and went to Amaria. 'For your troubles.' She handed her some coins.

Amaria curtseyed as she took the money. However miserable the conditions were for the ladies at Chinon, they were much worse in the maids' quarters. *Still*, thought Alice, *at least they are free to banter and play among themselves when their work is done.* She'd have preferred that to her present predicament of tiptoeing around, trying not to tread on royal toes — sensibilities being so taut at present.

The next morning, Alice woke to the sound of heavy rain crashing against the inadequate shutters. Too cold even to wash, Joanna and Alice dressed under the covers almost in darkness and hurried to join Marie for breakfast. Later, they'd return to attend Eleanor, but she'd requested not to be disturbed till after noon. Richard and his men had been riding through the night and were expected to arrive any time.

At Chinon, they were given rustic bread and peppered cheese for breakfast instead of pheasant drumsticks and quails' eggs, but at least the local ale was tasty due to the abundance of fresh water from the Loire.

The wind was beating the wooden door like a drum and prevented them from hearing the messenger knocking. They saw him only as he approached the table, mopping the excess rain from his face with one red hand and reaching inside his tunic for a parchment with the other. He hesitated, uncertain who to hand it to. Marie scrunched a cloth to quickly clean her hands before reaching for it. As she read, Alice scrutinized the messenger, whose short tunic identified him as one of the king's men.

Marie set the parchment down. 'The queen is sleeping still,' she said. 'Please tell the king that she was fatigued after waiting up for him last night and now she needs her rest. She shall attend him later with greatest pleasure.'

At midday the ladies went to check on Eleanor and found her sitting up, her head resting against the felt pillows, her expression troubled.

'Good to find you awake, Mother. I trust you slept well?'

Eleanor nodded. 'Sit,' she invited them.

'You should know that Henry sent a messenger to summon you to breakfast in his bedchamber ... alone,' Marie told her.

Eleanor smiled faintly and paled.

'I told him you were exhausted after waiting up so long for him last night,' Marie said.

'I have not shared my husband's bedchamber in an age,' Eleanor said. 'Thank God for sparing me that indignity at least, though I'm sure he'd not wish to lay a finger on me now that he has her!' She spat the last word. She was referring to Henry's mistress, Lady Rosamund, whom it was said he loved more than Eleanor. Her hand gripped Marie's. 'Any news of my sons?'

'Not yet, Mother,' Marie said, gently. 'But I'm sure they'll arrive presently.'

'In any case,' said Eleanor, 'it's time to rise. It sounds as though it's raining hard?'

'Very hard.'

Eleanor looked worried. 'I hope it does not impede the progress of my sons. I cannot withstand him alone.'

What a nightmare this is for her, Alice observed.

Dressed in a heavy turquoise brocade dress with a jewel-studded bodice, a thick gold collar around her neck and her hair covered with a lace veil, Eleanor descended with her ladies to pray awhile in the bleak chapel. Their maids held waxed sack cloths on sticks over their heads to protect them from the rain. They stayed so long in the chapel that Alice's toes went numb. Thankfully, the sound of horses' hooves and muffled shouts saved them from frostbite. Eleanor's face broke into a relieved smile, and she gathered her skirts and rushed out into the rain.

'Mother, in here, please!' Marie beckoned her into an archway for shelter.

The riders came into view, led by Richard and Geoffrey. Both were dressed in identical armour and helmets, but when they dismounted, Richard proved to be a great deal taller than his brother. Eleanor held out her arms to them and — despite their heavy armour — they ran to her like children.

Henry and his men were awaiting their arrival in the great hall — where fires had been lit since early morning. Henry appeared in the massive doorway, a shadow of his former self, and stood watching as the boys embraced their mother. He too held out his arms for them, but they hesitated, until Eleanor gave them a little push towards him.

'See how fine our sons are! How grown up they look in their coats of armour!' Henry cried, moved. 'Come, my queen, let's gather together before the fire.'

The maids rushed forward with their wax canopies as Eleanor and her ladies crossed the yard.

Alice and Joanna were occupied all evening pouring mead for the men, while Eleanor and Marie were engrossed in conversation. Alice was surprised by how little Geoffrey resembled either of his parents — being short and of slight build, with dark hair. His slanted eyes darted about uneasily, as if suspicious of his surroundings.

On Christmas Eve, Eleanor avoided spending time alone with Henry by claiming she was too preoccupied with preparations for next day. In fact, she entrusted others with decorating the halls and supervising the costumes, while she engaged her sons in urgent, whispered conversation about what had passed between them and Louis in Paris.

'He told me to demand Normandy,' Alice overheard Geoffrey tell Eleanor. 'My brothers were given titles at my age and therefore so should I.'

'Indeed you should, you deserve nothing less,' said Eleanor. 'However, we must wait till the time is right before broaching the subject with Henry. Your father, as you know, is touchy over these matters.'

'My father wishes to keep all the kingdom for himself,' said Geoffrey, petulantly.

'You were right, Mama,' said Richard. 'Louis gives the soundest advice. He says my older brother must insist that he and Louis' daughter are given their own kingdom to rule. He says he'll support them, no matter what it takes to achieve it.'

'That's good.' Eleanor's eyes met his in understanding. 'We need the kind of powerful support that Louis can offer if we hope to weaken Henry's hold and force him to hand power over to his sons.'

'Aquitaine shall be ours, Mama, if this comes to pass,' said Richard, passionately. 'It was your land by inheritance, and I'm determined it shall be yours again.'

'Oh, Richard.' Eleanor's eyes filled with tears. She looked at Geoffrey. 'My beloved sons! What would I do without you?'

'But you are right, Mama,' Richard said, 'we must tread carefully and not alert Father to our plans, or he will surely try to stop us. He is not amenable to sharing his territories. Strange, how clearly Louis seems to see what is due to us, but our own father does not.'

'He's too greedy and controlling,' offered Geoffrey.

'Your father's unyielding nature has caused no end of grief,' Eleanor said, bitterly. 'We know there is no use in attempting to reason with him, for he is so unbending.' She considered a moment, then said, slowly, deliberately, 'We must therefore take what is rightfully ours by whatever subtle means necessary.'

'I agree, Mama.'

'So do I,' Geoffrey chimed in.

During the conversation, Alice was practically holding her breath. *Treason.* And she was witness to it, she thought, fearfully. What a strange family, the mother and sons plotting with the ex-husband against the father while living under the same roof! No wonder Marie was so distracted, she realised. What did Joanna's inappropriate love-affair matter under these dangerous conditions? Alice couldn't bear to think what would happen if Henry discovered what was transpiring behind his back.

Christmas Day passed without incident. By now, Alice was accustomed to the prolonged, often farcical, entertainment preferred by Henry and would usually escape early to bed. On one such occasion, Marie followed her to the bedchamber so they were alone together.

'Alice? May I speak with you?' Marie called, untying her boots and lying down on Eleanor's grand bed.

Alice was behind the curtain about to undress, but she emerged to sit with her. 'Of course you may,' she said, gently.

'I am so afraid!' Marie said, bursting into tears.

'There now, don't cry.' Alice stroked her hair. 'Please, don't cry, it is not so bad.'

'Oh, Alice, these are terrible times in which to live, I fear!'

Alice brushed some loose strands of hair from Marie's forehead. She felt Marie's breath on her arm.

'I'm afraid our world may be about to fall apart, due to Mother's ambition.'

Alice nodded, gravely.

'Nothing is secure now,' said Marie. 'My family has begun to eat itself from the inside, like a worm in the pith.'

Alice dared not speak.

'I am afraid for our lives and … I fear I shall have to return to my husband,' said Marie.

'Would that be so terrible?'

'Oh, yes! I dread to think of it. We had such lofty ambitions for our court at Poitiers, and now we risk losing everything… Our troubadours and court of love… My work with Chretien. It's unbearable to imagine leaving it all unfinished, only to be holed up with a man I barely know…'

Alice was shocked at how little regard Marie seemed to have for her husband. She wondered, then, if there was some romantic attachment between Marie and Chretien. The thought pierced through her heart like a lance and she paled. Her voice shook when she spoke. 'Would you rather be married to Chretien?'

Marie laughed. 'Goodness, no! Such an idea!'

'My apologies...'

'Why don't you get undressed and come under the covers?' Marie suggested. 'Then we can speak into the night, if we wish...'

Such an invitation warmed Alice's blood with both fear and excitement.

Marie misread her hesitation. 'Only if you want to...'

What am I to her? Alice wondered, undressing in the candlelight. *Would she think of me with regret if we were parted?* She arranged herself carefully in bed before snuffing the candle. 'Do you not confide in your husband?' probed Alice, boldly.

'I cannot confide in anyone the way I confide in you!'

In the darkness, Alice smiled.

'Please understand, my husband is not a bad man, it's just he doesn't share my values or ambitions... Yes, I too am ambitious, like my mother, though my interests are not political.'

'Perhaps you'll not have to return to your husband,' suggested Alice. 'Perhaps all will go according to plan and our court will continue to thrive.'

'Oh, I dearly hope so! These past five years at Poitiers have been the happiest I've ever known.'

'Well, then, let's hope for the best.'

Alice was thoughtful. She realised they'd been the best years of her life, too, despite the trouble with Joanna. Her friendship with Marie had brought so much joy, as well as some anguish. She wondered what on earth would become of them, if things went badly and Eleanor — with her ladies — had to leave the court at Poitiers. She had no husband to return to and neither did Joanna, now. She would have broached the subject with Marie, but she heard her gentle snoring. She kissed her cheek, very softly, before slipping back to her own bed.

CHAPTER TWENTY-FOUR

Flooding on the tracks meant Eleanor and her ladies were forced to abandon their carriage and ride astride like the men-at-arms, dressed in thick tunics and pants on the journey home. The watchmen regarded them suspiciously at first as they entered Poitiers, not recognising them.

Chretien and some other noblemen had prepared the homecoming banquet and — after peeling off their men's garments and washing away the grime of Chinon — the ladies changed into fresh silks and descended, happy to be home. Relieved of the tension Henry's presence invoked, Eleanor's mood became gay.

After the banquet, the ladies watched the courtiers dance, too fatigued to join in themselves. Alice's eyes began to droop and even Joanna was pensive.

'Why so quiet, Joanna?' asked Eleanor. 'It is not like you. Why do you not dance?'

Alice's ears pricked up nervously and she was suddenly wide awake.

'I am a little weary,' replied Joanna.

'Weary? A young lady of vigorous health such as you? Nonsense! I know that look. I've seen that look before on many a maid. It is love-weariness you suffer from, is it not?'

A pained smile betrayed Joanna's guilt.

'Now, Alice, don't be worried,' said Eleanor, noticing her serious expression.

Marie caught her eye in sympathy and cleared her throat. 'Alice is just lamenting Joanna's broken engagement,' she said.

'It is quite natural she should grieve… Such offers don't grow on trees, even for one as beautiful as Joanna.'

Eleanor turned serious. She spoke low so only they could hear. 'Dear Alice, dear Joanna, I feel in some way responsible for what happened with the knight, for it was I who delayed the wedding. Had we not delayed, then you would be Lady Joanna de Montel by now. Please know that I intend to do whatever I can to make amends for your loss.'

Alice clung to the words like a drowning person to a rope, thanking the queen extensively. Eleanor had always protected them and now they were left with no choice but to place their trust entirely in her.

Secret ambassadors between Louis' court in Paris and Eleanor of Aquitaine carried messages informing them of Henry's movements. On returning from Paris, young king Henry had demanded he be given either England, Normandy or Anjou, as Louis had suggested. Henry refused and — suspecting that Louis was trying to influence him — had insisted that young Henry accompany him at all times, so he could keep an eye on him.

The young king complained bitterly to Louis about a recent trip to Montferrand, where Henry had made him assist in negotiating a marriage for their youngest child, John, who was only six years old. As his unofficial title suggested, John 'lackland' had been intended for the Church and had passed his infancy at Fontevrault, but Henry had suddenly changed his mind and withdrawn him, determined that the youngest should have his own inheritance. Henry had subsequently arranged a match between John and Count Humbert of Maurienne's heiress, but he promised the Count that John would receive three strategic castles in the Loire, including Chinon, Loudon and Mirabeau.

The young king was outraged that a younger brother would receive a part of his inheritance and was also deeply hurt by Henry's apparent preference for John.

Eleanor read the following part of Louis' letter aloud to her ladies: 'The young king says Henry has even taken steps to dismiss certain members of his household that he believes are a bad influence — thus treating my son-in-law and daughter like irresponsible children. However, I have written to advise my son-in-law to conceal his resentment from Henry, in case he grows suspicious. The young king replied to say he would do my bidding, but says he does not know if he can hold out much longer without rebelling. He says he is nothing more than a powerless pawn in his father's game at chess. Therefore, Duchess, I advise you to write to your son and encourage him to temperance, as I have done.'

Eleanor rose and paced about while her ladies remained silent and fearful.

'Please call Richard to me, alone,' she ordered, then, 'and tell Amaria to bring a quill and parchment.'

Eleanor and Richard drafted a careful letter to her eldest son at Winchester, in which they stressed the need for patience. 'Henry must be kept in ignorance of our movements until our supporters are mobilized, otherwise we may fail to force his hand.'

Eleanor was dressing for the banquet, her ladies in attendance, when the reply came from young Henry. Dressed in an undershift as pale as her skin, her loose hair glowing russet like autumn leaves, the queen untied the parchment with nervous, trembling hands.

'Do sit, Mother,' Marie suggested softly, taking Eleanor's hand and drawing her down beside her. Next to Marie's full form and face, Eleanor looked willowy and fae.

'Would you read it, my flower?' Eleanor suggested. 'My hands are shaking…'

Marie took it from her.

'You may read it aloud.'

How solid and reliable is Marie, thought Alice, *how loyal are all of Eleanor's children to her.*

'Most esteemed queen and mother,' Marie began, 'forgive me for writing first to Louis, but I was desperate for the advice of a general. I collapsed with exhaustion after returning from Montferrand with Henry. Imagine how bitterly disappointed I was to learn that my younger brother would receive three great estates — Chinon, oh, Chinon included! My heart breaks as I write. Should not these be part of my inheritance?'

'Yes! Of course!' said Eleanor. 'Go on.'

'Not anticipating such a base move, I found myself completely at a loss and unable to defend myself. Initially, when Father insisted I travel with him, I harboured some hope that at last he intended to bestow some territory on me. Never would I have dreamt that he intended showering my brother with such gifts and leaving me bereft. I ask you, Mother, was I not crowned king before the world and God? What madness, then, is this which my old father succumbs to? Even as I write, I am shaking with rage. I'd drag him from his court and tear the grey beard from his chin had I not pledged my secrecy to Louis, and now to you.

'I solemnly give my word to do nothing which would cause Henry to become suspicious, but I do not know for how long I can hold out. I think of us riding towards Montferrand that morning through fields of young lavender, the sun warm on our backs; how hopeful was I that Henry was about to do his duty by me at last. When instead he gave away three of my castles, I felt such loss, like a great void opened up inside me and is, I fear, filling fast with hate.'

'I know the void well,' said Eleanor, 'and the rotten stuff that fills it.' She bowed her head, her slight shoulders slumped. A moaning sound came from somewhere within, like a wounded animal.

'Call Richard at once,' said Marie, urgently. 'Mother, are you well?'

Eleanor whispered something. Marie leant in closer to her. 'My children...' she was saying, 'my children...'

'We are here, Mother. Richard is coming.'

'Oh, Marie, my wonderful Marie, how capable you are. How proud I am of you! My heart breaks for my children, for I know not what is to become of you.'

'We are here, Mother, we are safe.'

'But you, Marie, you are always by my side like an angel.'

Richard entered. 'Mama, what news from our brother?' He stopped abruptly when he saw Eleanor with her head hanging. Marie put a warning finger to her lips and handed him the parchment so he could read it for himself.

'But this is good news?' Richard said, confused by his mother's sorrowful aspect.

'Yes,' Eleanor whispered, tears trickling down her face. 'Henry is tearing us apart. He is doing to his son what he did to Thomas Becket — he is killing him — not by his own hand, but by his reckless actions. Why does he not learn?'

'Then we must stop him,' said Richard, firmly. 'I'll take Geoffrey with me to Paris to mobilize our supporters. It is time.'

'Yes, it is time,' Eleanor said, quietly. After Richard left, she turned to Marie, her expression sad and apologetic. 'I'm afraid the Loire will run red with blood before this quarrel is resolved. Our court of love is turned to one of hate.'

Marie's eyes brimmed with tears. 'I shall continue to support you, Mother, in times of sorrow as well as joy.'

The next day, Eleanor rose early to see her sons off on their journey to Paris. Afterwards, her ladies joined her in the brightest chamber of the Tower to sort through the discarded remnants of her sons' wardrobes, strewn across the oak table.

'The weather gets colder at night in Paris and it's much damper than here, so I advised them to wear layers of wool under their armour,' Eleanor said, lovingly folding one of Richard's tunics. She seemed restored to her old self. It being a bright, spring day, she suggested they take a walk to the rose garden.

Joanna had cast her dark woollen dress aside in favour of a fresh new linen of pale blue. Alice glanced with disapproval at the light dress, afraid Joanna would catch cold. She herself clung to her habitual black, her greying hair tucked into a wimple with a stiff headdress, stark against her aging skin. She could not cast aside the fears of yesterday so easily, and her face was grave and thoughtful.

A new carpet of brilliant green grass had grown up on the lawn, with rows of pretty pansies fluttering round the edges. Fat, fertile buds had broken out along the thorny desert of roses and the stems were running with fresh green juice.

The ladies sat on the stone bench, basking in the sun. They passed burgundy grapes between them, enjoying the tangy skin and the juice bursting in their mouths. After a while, a messenger came to say that Bertran de Born had arrived in court and was seeking an interview with Eleanor.

'Tell him to come here directly,' Eleanor ordered. Bertran had spent many months at young Henry's court in Winchester, so he was sure to bring news.

'Bertran de Born,' announced the messenger.

Bertran entered, resplendent in a velvet green tunic and pants. He kissed Eleanor's delicate hand, then bowed to the ladies. 'Lady Marie, Lady Joanna, Lady...'

'Alice, Lady Alice,' prompted Eleanor.

Alice shrank from his amused glance.

'Take a seat,' offered Marie, moving so he could sit next to Eleanor.

'To what do we owe so great a pleasure?' Eleanor began. 'Do you bring news ... from overseas?'

Bertran sighed dramatically and closed his eyes against the sun. 'Yes. I have just returned from the young king's court at Winchester. I resided there for nine months and I'm happy to report that your son is the most marvellous host. He is both generous and extravagant in his tastes and offers the best of everything to his knights. I passed some of the gayest hours of my life under his roof.'

'I'm sure my son appreciates your contribution to his court, Bertran. I am not ignorant of your singular talents.'

He bowed. 'I am sorry to report that the old king has ordered many of your son's closest knights to leave, as he doesn't trust them. Insufferable insult to the young king ... and also to myself, for I was one of those knights ordered to leave.'

Joanna smirked. Alice too was secretly pleased, for she still grieved over the trouble that pair had caused her niece.

'How does my son, Bertran?' Eleanor asked.

'He is frustrated, my lady. He has grown very unhappy, in fact. His father's actions have rendered him powerless and hopeless. Something must be done,' Bertran hissed. 'I came today to tell you that my men and I are at your service, should we be needed.'

'Thank you, Bertran, you shall be needed, and soon. Richard and Geoffrey have already gone to Louis in Paris.'

'Very good, my lady. I must not linger any longer, as my men are waiting at the gates.' Bertran took Eleanor's hands in his and squeezed them tightly. His voice became choked with emotion. 'He ... your son ... my cherished friend, has grown so distressed that I'm afraid this business will make him seriously ill.' He left abruptly, blinded by his tears.

'How extraordinary,' remarked Marie. 'I've never seen Bertran so moved.'

'Bertran is not all bad. My son has many great admirers, remember,' said Eleanor, thoughtfully. 'He could have a great following, if given the chance. Hopefully he shall have his moment soon.'

CHAPTER TWENTY-FIVE

On the first of March, Eleanor and her ladies were going to picnic in the woods when a messenger rode up, halting before them. His short mantle distinguished him as one of Henry's men. Eleanor cast them a worried glance before taking the parchment from him.

'Hail, our worthy queen,' she read. 'Our eldest son, recently crowned the young king, has shown some wayward traits of late I fear must be corrected. I have therefore taken it upon myself to instruct him on eradicating certain undesirable elements of his character, starting with a tendency to disrespect his father. Being only seventeen winters old — as yet of tender age — we may hope to righten these faults and steer him to better guidance. Those supporters about him who have filled his head with rebellious, grandiose ideas have been thinned out like weeds from the flowerbeds of my son's court at Winchester. One such fellow being the troubadour, Bertran de Born, whom I've banished back to Poitou, not as benign as a weed, but rather a fully poisonous plant in terms of influence over our son.

'The young king shall remain firmly planted by my side until I am convinced he is on the correct path. He shall learn from my example as we travel together through my kingdom, eating from my plate, drinking from my cup, sleeping in my bed. Soon, I hope, he shall beat correctly, in tandem with his father. I do not speak ill of our son, but as yet he shows himself unfit to rule a kingdom, being overgenerous with his silver and underrating his father's advice. He lacks the calculating thrift and political shrewdness of our second son, Duke Richard of

Aquitaine, but he possesses a rare charm that Richard lacks. I've been proud witness to the fervent following that our eldest son inspires through his grace. I am determined he shall make a fine king as a result of my corrective measures.

'I mean to embark for Chinon tomorrow, where I shall sojourn until the summer's end. From there, young Henry and I shall travel to Poitou and our other lands to oversee affairs. We shall look forward to a reunion with our queen and other sons over the coming months. Affectionately, your loving Henry.'

Eleanor surged with anger. 'He means to interfere with our barons yet again.' The news gave her a burst of nervous energy and she marched ahead of her ladies to the picnic area. 'Nobody destroys my peace of mind as effectively as Henry,' Eleanor sighed.

'At least he doesn't suspect any involvement on your part, Mother,' remarked Marie.

One evening, just over a week later, Alice happened to be gazing out of the window at the roses when the king's messenger came galloping at great speed down the avenue. His sense of urgency immediately filled her with dread.

'Joanna?' Alice called. 'Come, we must go to Eleanor.'

They bumped into Marie, also rushing down the stairwell, and proceeded without a word. Never before had they seen the Tower door wide open, and they paused to stare in shock at it. Some men-at-arms had gathered around the queen, in case the news proved threatening.

The men stood back as Eleanor's ladies surrounded her.

'Yes,' Eleanor murmured, after reading the letter that had been delivered to her. 'Yes.' She handed it to Marie.

'What does it say?' asked Joanna, unable to bear the tension.

'It is from Henry,' Eleanor said. 'The young king escaped from the bed he shared with his father in Chinon on the night of the 7th of March...'

Alice gasped. Joanna squeezed her hand.

'Henry writes that he made the guards drunk with some fortified wine he found in the cellar. The same wine served to him and his men by the queen at Christmas...' Eleanor had blanched and looked ill. It was clear that Henry had begun to suspect her involvement.

'Where did young Henry flee to?' asked Joanna. 'Perhaps he just wished to return to his bride at Winchester? That is not so bad...'

'I'm afraid not,' said Marie. 'At first he went North, to Normandy, which makes it look like he did indeed intend to cross the channel to England, but then he changed his mind and went to Paris. Henry writes that he intends to take refuge with King Louis.'

The messenger addressed Eleanor. 'The king wonders, Duchess, why the young king would fly from his own father to the protection of Louis of France, the Duchess's erstwhile-husband? He wonders what you know of this, Duchess?' He stood, staring, awaiting Eleanor's response.

'My mother knows nothing of this,' said Marie, sternly. 'Why should she? The young king was with the old king these past months, and now he is with the French king.'

'The king also wonders, Duchess,' said the messenger, stubbornly ignoring Marie, 'where are your other sons?'

'You have delivered your message and now you must leave,' ordered Eleanor.

'Do you insult a messenger of the king?'

'I do. Get off my land or I shall place you in irons for your insolence!'

It was unlike Eleanor to be so direct and confrontational. This was an open declaration of something akin to war between herself and Henry.

The messenger blinked, taking a step back. 'Duchess, let me warn you, I shall soon return, and I'll not be alone.'

'Go, you miserable, cowardly wretch!' Eleanor turned to her knights. 'We must leave for Paris without delay. Henry's troops may be marching even as we speak. Do you think the old ox-tracks are dry enough after winter? If so, we can use them to get through the Loire. If we can get to Louis' court unmolested and be reunited with my sons, we may still stand a chance of defeating Henry.' She turned to address Marie and her ladies. 'So, my cherished ones —' her tone was sad but resolved — 'this is it. I cannot ask you to attend me any further on this perilous path. I must go on alone. Come, help me prepare, and then we must say goodbye…'

Marie looked at Alice. 'I shall accompany her,' she said, bravely.

'So shall I,' said Joanna, quickly.

'And I,' agreed Alice.

They smiled at each other and embraced as a threesome.

'Bless you all,' whispered Eleanor.

'It's the least we can do, my lady,' said Alice, 'after all you have done for us. We are not the least bit afraid.'

A messenger was dispatched to Fontevrault, informing the abbess of their flight.

'We'll travel through the night and, hopefully, take a few hours rest at Fontevrault before going on to Paris,' Eleanor told her ladies. 'The most important thing is to create some distance tonight between ourselves and Henry's men.'

Despite the solemnity of the occasion, they chortled with merriment as they changed into their disguises. They were hoping to pass for a party of knights. Eleanor's best maid, Amaria, was to travel with them. Always so pristine, she looked neat even as a knight, her tunic tucked neatly into her trousers under an armoured vest and her face scrubbed and shining under her helmet. Luckily, they were experienced enough riders to ride astride like men — all except Amaria.

By midnight, they were ready and the grooms brought their mares out into the courtyard. Not wishing to alert the court to their departure, the women spoke in hushed voices, and even the horses seemed to intuit the need for secrecy, stepping delicately with their hooves.

The knights led the women expertly via the old ox-tracks, which were unused except by farmers herding livestock. They rode throughout the night, reaching Fontevrault just as dawn broke, sending eerie fingers of light over the massive stone structure.

At Fontevrault, their message had been received and they were ushered straight to the abbess's chambers. Even at that hour, the abbess was dressed in full habit and stiff veil, her giant crucifix dangling from its chain. She crushed Eleanor to her bosom. 'Duchess,' she said. 'May the Lord deliver you.'

The abbess arranged for a rich meal to be served to them in a luxurious apartment, carried in by a host of discreet nuns, on their way to morning prayer. Eleanor did not join them, but sat apart while they ate, whispering in serious undertones with the abbess. After eating, they all slept together in a grand bed, reserved for visiting royalty.

After what seemed like a few moments, they were woken and urged to dress quickly. With the light quickly turning up on the day, they departed again for Paris.

Many of the old tracks to Paris were impassable, so they were forced to use the main road. They were, however, hopeful that they had placed enough distance between themselves and Henry's men.

The day turned hot, and the ladies perspired under their heavy woollen livery. Thankfully, they'd not carried any other clothes or baggage for fear of attracting attention. They brought only leather flasks of ale and mutton, wrapped in their saddlebags, as was customary for knights.

'My goodness,' Marie panted. 'I'm looking forward to a nice soak once we get to Father's palace. I'll happily walk about wrapped in a sheet like a Roman before squeezing into these stuffy clothes again! How can they suffer such oppressive garments?' Marie's voluptuous figure was bulging out of the livery, and she looked most uncomfortable.

'You'll not be forced to wear a sheet, my flower,' Eleanor said. 'We shall all have new silk dresses made up by Louis' Parisian dressmaker.'

'How marvellous,' exclaimed Joanna. 'Is she very skilled?'

'The very best,' Eleanor replied.

'I suppose we could be made to reside indefinitely at the palace?' wondered Marie.

'Yes, it's likely,' Eleanor agreed. 'I expect it could take many, many months before this is resolved.'

They spoke so confidently, Alice thought, that it was as though they'd already arrived.

'I've always wished to see Paris!' exclaimed Joanna.

'Well, now you shall,' Eleanor said, smiling.

Alice was worried about the things they'd left behind and whether they'd be safe. What if Henry's troops set up camp in the Tower, laid their grubby hands on their fine things and took them as presents for their whores? The Parisian court was elegant, the height of sophistication, and she worried she would be despised. Joanna would soon win them over with her considerable beauty and talent, but they'd find Alice strange. She feared they'd mock her Southern accent and her ugliness.

They stopped by the roadside to drink the pail of milk that had been given to them at Fontevrault, but they found that it had soured in the sun. By nightfall, they were exhausted, their muscles aching, but they dared not stop for fear that Henry's men were close on their heels.

'We must brave on through the night,' Eleanor advised. The knights agreed. 'Hopefully by morning we'll have reached Paris, but we must exercise extreme caution passing through the gates, for Henry's guards will surely be on the lookout.'

The danger inherent in the sentence silenced and sobered all of them, and Alice worried about what was to come.

They travelled all night through dark, unfamiliar countryside. At dawn, the city of Chartres came into view, and they knew they were close to Paris. So far, no one had given them so much as a second glance.

As their horses skirted the cobblestones outside the town, they passed a bakery with baskets of freshly baked wheaten loaves temptingly arranged. The aroma was maddening.

'Perhaps we could take a short break,' suggested Eleanor.

The party grew instantly more cheerful. They halted underneath some elm trees, with delicate, baby leaves covering the branches. Dismounting, they stretched their limbs and groaned with soreness.

The knights uncorked the ale and passed it around.

'Amaria.' Eleanor handed the maid some silver. 'Go and buy a basket of loaves.'

When Amaria went inside, another group of knights rode up, halting outside the bakery, apparently with the same idea. Eleanor's party glanced nervously at one another.

'We should not have stopped,' Eleanor muttered.

The party outnumbered them by scores. Alice saw them look over at Eleanor's group, examining their livery, curiously. Some of them entered the bakery behind Amaria.

Alice saw one of them come out and whisper something in their captain's ear. Frowning, he turned to scrutinize them, this time suspiciously. At that moment, Amaria emerged, innocently, with her basket of loaves. They mounted in a hurry and were about to gallop off when they were stopped.

'Halt!' the captain ordered. 'Which one is your captain?' He looked at Eleanor as he spoke.

'I am captain here,' she answered.

'We have reason to believe you have a maid in your party, disguised as a knight. We have been ordered by King Henry to report any suspicious activity hereabouts.' He pointed to Amaria. 'Ask him to remove his helmet.'

Amaria froze.

'That won't be necessary,' said Eleanor. 'I can vouch for her. Yes, you are right, she is a maid. Is it not safer for a maid to disguise herself for safety among so many men?'

'Dismount, all of you,' the knight ordered. 'Remove your helmets.'

They were caught. It seemed as unreal as a nightmare.

Eleanor dismounted first and slowly removed her helmet.

The men gasped as her magnificent hair came tumbling down. They recognised her at once as Eleanor of Aquitaine. The captain drew breath through his teeth. Many of them bent on one knee before her, but their captain cast them a disdainful look.

'This lady is a traitor!'

Eleanor stood tall, like a goddess in her armour.

'Eleanor of Aquitaine, you are under arrest by order of the king.'

'Which king?' she said, ironically.

'Have you not heard?' said the captain. 'Your son, Henry, was captured as he entered Paris. His troops were defeated in Normandy. It is over, Duchess.'

A messenger was dispatched to Henry, while the knights kept watch over Eleanor.

Eleanor's ladies were too crushed, too sad to speak. They'd come so close. Joanna burst into tears, but Alice shushed her. 'We must be brave,' she whispered. 'This is the path we chose, and we must face it.'

'I'm not concerned for us,' Joanna said, her voice distorted with grief. 'What is to become of Eleanor?'

Alice cradled Joanna in her arms and rocked her back and forth.

'Some party of knights,' snickered one of Henry's men.

'Come, ladies, we must keep up our strength,' Eleanor called. Amaria, too, was crying softly. 'No one is to blame,' Eleanor soothed. 'Dry those tears.' She broke the bread, sharing it out among them. 'At least we were caught next to a fine patisserie,' she joked in an attempt to make them smile.

Night drew in early, and they huddled up with their backs to their horses to keep warm, Henry's men observing their every move.

'Lady!' one of them called to Joanna. 'What is your name?'

'My name is none of your affair,' Joanna snapped.

'Suit yourself,' the man snorted. 'We only wanted to make friends.'

'I'd rather not make friends with the enemy!' she said.

217

'That's enough, Joanna,' Alice cautioned. 'Just ignore them.'

At last, the messenger returned from Henry who, it seemed, was still in Chinon.

The captain took the parchment and read aloud: 'The Duchess must be placed in irons overnight until the king makes up his mind what to do with her.'

Eleanor laughed. 'That could take some time!'

As they bound Eleanor of Aquitaine's slender hands and her feet with chains, the men fearfully avoided looking at her face. Finally, the captain came himself to hang an iron bar from her neck, so she could no longer stand, but fell forward onto her knees.

Alice and the other ladies cried out in protest but were pushed aside with a warning.

'You may stay with her tonight, if you wish, or you may go to the devil for all I care!' roared the captain. 'But if you cause any more trouble, you too shall be placed in irons!'

The men left to set up a tent nearby. Eleanor's ladies lit a small fire, which they kept burning throughout the night.

'Alice, Joanna, come close,' Eleanor said. 'You must listen carefully to what I have to say. When I am taken — for taken I shall be — you must go to Fontevrault and wait there for me. I have left provision for you with the abbess, enough to last a lifetime. You shall reside in the royal chambers until such time as I am free to join you. It is all arranged. Joanna, they have much need of skilled hawkers for their forests and Alice, you must continue to protect your niece. Promise you'll do as I ask.'

'I promise,' Joanna said.

'Alice…' Marie looked into her eyes, intensely. 'I shall be able to come visit you at Fontevrault.'

'I promise too,' said Alice. Her heart was beating fiercely with anxiety and a strange excitement, too. She wondered if they'd even make it to Fontevrault, or if they'd all be hanged.

Henry's men came next morning with further orders from the king.

'Duchess Eleanor of Aquitaine is to be taken to Chinon, where she is to be interrogated and immured indefinitely in one of the Towers.'

'Well, it could be worse,' Eleanor said. 'I've been my husband's prisoner all my life; what difference does it make which Tower I am imprisoned in? The court at Poitiers was only a brief illusion of freedom, but the walls were already caving in...'

'Take her over here,' ordered the captain.

The men half-walked, half-carried Eleanor to a horse, pushing her up on the saddle, behind its rider.

'She can ride her own horse, surely?' Marie cried. Alice placed a cautionary hand on her shoulder.

'The deuce she can,' said the captain, laughing darkly. 'That horse looks like Pegasus. I'll not risk her sailing up into the heavens halfway to Chinon! Strap her legs down!' he barked. 'Good and tight!'

'Joanna!' Eleanor called to the weeping girl. 'Promise me you'll never lose your freedom, as I lost mine.'

'I promise.'

The captain consulted his parchment, muttering to himself, 'The Duchess may take her maid, Amaria with her, but she'll not need any attending-ladies, where she's going. Lady Marie must be escorted back to her husband, the Count of Champagne... Come, Lady, you may ride your own mare.'

'Oh, Marie!' Alice rushed to her and kissed her neck.

Marie held her in a tight embrace and they cried together. 'Don't concern yourself, Alice, I expected this. I am ready,' she whispered.

'Come, that's enough, we don't have all day!' roared the captain.

'I'll find you as soon as I can!' said Marie, urgently.

'I shall be waiting, always!' Alice replied. Only at the very last minute did they let go of each other's hands.

Henry's troops disappeared quickly from sight, leaving Alice and Joanna alone, but together in their loss. Only a scattering of Eleanor's knights had remained to escort them safely to Fontevrault.

Joanna's disconsolate weeping made it impossible for her to ride, so Alice had the knights lift Joanna up behind her, on her dappled mare, while Joanna's smoky one ran alongside. Joanna's arms hugged Alice, and her tears soaked through Alice's back.

The night was mild and hung with splendid stars and, despite the appalling turn of events, Alice felt both strong and determined. She would protect Joanna, as Eleanor had said, and they would survive.

Joanna's breathing deepened into sleep and Alice was overcome with gratitude and clarity. From somewhere deep in the trees, a nightingale's sweet and mournful singing made Alice smile and weep at once.

Before dawn, the oak forests of Fontevrault came into view and only then did Alice feel her tiredness. The Abbess would be waiting for them and Marie had promised to visit. Alice's neck was still tingling from where Marie had kissed her, and her heart was filled with hope.

A NOTE TO THE READER

Dear Reader,

Thanks so much for taking the time to read this book.

I was always fascinated by the character of Eleanor of Aquitaine; her bravery and spirit of adventure, that freedom to be herself in that period. I was introduced to the lyrics of the troubadours while doing my MA in 2006 and became intrigued by the elusive concept of courtly love. That Eleanor presided over 'courts' or 'games' of love is unlikely, however, her court at Poitiers was certainly a place where troubadours flocked and flourished, sumptuous costumes (and fantastic shoes) were worn, love affairs (surely) happened and poetry and music prevailed for a brief time, before Eleanor's arrest and the horrors of the Albigensian crusade invaded Southern France. She was a Duchess who (I like to think) shows how good it gets when women become rulers. Even after years of imprisonment in England, she emerged with her spirit intact, energised to fight her cause.

I used whatever sketchy details are known of Eleanor, Henry II, their sons and daughter and other historical personages to draw fuller portraits of their personalities, but of course these are open to interpretation. I have tried to be true to historical events, diplomatic relations, places and timelines, but please forgive any errors! I am indebted to Alison Weir's non-fiction account in *Eleanor of Aquitaine* (2000) for the description of the murder of Thomas Becket. My fictitious characters and leading ladies, namely Alice and Joanna, I can vouch for by saying they are always true to character.

I hope you enjoy the book. It is a huge privilege for me to have you read it. I would be so grateful if you let us know what you think by leaving a review on **Amazon** or **Goodreads**. You can also contact me directly on my website: **www.coirlemooney.com**. Many, many thanks again.

Coirle

Sapere Books is an exciting new publisher of brilliant fiction and popular history.

To find out more about our latest releases and our monthly bargain books visit our website:
saperebooks.com

Made in United States
North Haven, CT
14 July 2023

39037362R00124